PRAISE FOR

Connected Fates, Separate Destinies

"With *Connected Fates, Separate Destinies*, Marine provides all of us with a map to help orient ourselves within the web of our origin stories."

— Ruby Warrington, author of *Sober Curious*

"*Connected Fates, Separate Destinies* is a powerful, potent, and magical book that will help you recognize the hidden patterns in your life that make the biggest difference, so you can clear them once and for all and live a life of greater peace and acceptance. I highly recommend this book for every single person on the planet."

— Sahara Rose, best-selling author of *Discover Your Dharma*

"Marine Sélénée offers enlightened wisdom and practical tools to make peace with your past and create your dream future, through Family Constellations therapy. Now, more than ever, we all need to fall madly in love with ourselves and after reading this book, you will be well on your way."

— Sah D'Simone, author of *Spiritually Sassy* and *5-Minute Daily Meditations*

"Marine Sélénée has a true gift. *Connected Fates, Separate Destinies* gracefully guides you to your highest source of healing, which is found when you seek within. This book provides a mirror to seeing your highest self, and learning to honor your lineage through love, care, and reverence."

— Rosie Acosta, author, yoga and meditation teacher, and host of the *Radically Loved* podcast

"Marine offers a fascinating picture of family constellations and its hidden energetic structures within the family system. In short, she explains that whatever we reject is what we repeat. This book is an offering to your soul that will compel you to rewrite your story, accept your family, and break the cycle once and for all. As Marine's client and friend, I enthusiastically endorse her teachings and guidance. Pay attention to this book because there is so much to learn here."

— Bee Bosnak, spiritual teacher and business mentor

Broken Bottles

Broken Bottles

Anthony Koranda

Tortoise Books
Chicago

FIRST EDITION, APRIL, 2023

Published in the United States by Tortoise Books
www.tortoisebooks.com

ASIN: B0BFMGZT27
ISBN-13: 978-1-948954-73-0

Cover Design: Gerald Brennan

For my wife

Contents

Roger

As far as I was concerned, Roger was my father, even if he refused to admit anything close to paternity. He never said it to me directly, but I laid awake at night, listening to him and my mother have the same argument in the living room, Roger's voice pushing through the door.

"He looks nothing like me," Roger said with a rattle in his throat, gruff from years of smoking.

"What do you mean?" my mother said. "We fucked exactly nine months before he was born." I heard the flick of her lighter, hissing butane, smelled the airy smoke of a light cigarette wafting through the crack in my door.

"Bullshit," Roger said. "I was on a fucking minesweeper so deep in the Persian Gulf we couldn't even get skin mags delivered, much less knock you up," he said, and I imagined the tan skin of his face, marked with creases, folding like old leather. His graying mustache twitching like it always did when he got angry. I closed my eyes, imagined him standing over my mother, both palms flat on the table, arms stiff, his navy tattoos fading from all the time spent in the sun on construction sites.

"What do you want me to tell you?" my mother said. "You're the only one I fucked so it's gotta be yours."

I shifted my body, turned to the wall, studied the Garfield calendar hanging above my bed, the one Roger bought me last New Year's. It was two weeks until my tenth birthday. I pulled the pillow over my head, smelled the heat of my breath, and thought about what it would be like if Roger wanted me, admitted he was my father. I breathed deep, heavy and hot into the old fabric. I wouldn't call him Roger anymore, or 'Sir' when he got really pissed. One day, I would just call him Dad.

St. Jude

Detective Knapczyk worked on the gang and drug task force. Roger liked him because he was Polish and fat and jolly, a beard as thick as shag carpet covering his face. He also said it was a good idea to have a friend who's a cop, that you never know when you may need a favor.

Knapczyk drove around the neighborhood in an unmarked silver Caprice, handing out his card to the guys on Sunnyside or Wilson or Leland. "Call me," he told them. "Let's stop the killing around here," and they'd crumple the card in their fists and drop it in the gutter as Knapczyk waddled back to his car, slumped into the driver's seat so heavy his girth squeaked the shocks.

Knapczyk lived on 31st Street, a long way from home. All his neighbors were cops and firemen. Roger always said he didn't know how Knapczyk got the money for such a big house on a policeman's salary. "He's got his hand in somebody's pocket," Roger said. I was never sure whose pocket it was.

I sat in the dining room at Knapczyk's house, the sun pouring in from bay windows that faced the street, huge oak table stretching from one wall to the other. Roger always insisted taking the furthest seat at one end of the table, Knapczyk on the other end. "The king's seat," Roger called it. They were so far apart they had to yell at each other to have a conversation. I don't think Knapczyk could hear half of what Roger was saying. He just smiled and laughed and blew clouds of smoke from the Marlboro Red that always hung from his lips.

I sat in the middle of the table, my back to the bay windows, smoke pushing in from both sides. In the DARE program at school a couple weeks before, someone came in and showed our class pictures of a smoker's lungs, old and shriveled, like a beat-up rubber balloon that lost its air. I thought of what the smoke was doing to my lungs as Roger and Knapczyk puffed away.

On the wall across the table, there was a portrait that was supposed to look like the Last Supper, but in place of Jesus and Paul and Judas and the others, there were all these men in pinstripe suits. I was old enough to recognize Don Corleone from *The Godfather* sitting in place of Jesus, but I wasn't quite sure of the others.

"Who's in the photo?" I asked Knapczyk when there was lull in their shouting.

"It's not a photo," Knapczyk said, taking another drag. "It's a painting. I paid a lot of money for it because it's a painting. Not a photo."

"Oh," I said, looking back to Roger who was now studying the painting with his head cocked to the side. "So who's in the painting?"

"Gangsters," Knapczyk said.

"From the movies, right?"

"That's right, kid."

"I thought you were a cop?" I asked.

"I am a cop," Knapczyk unclipped his badge from his waist and held it up. "See," and he wiggled it from side to side.

"So, if you're a cop, why do you have a painting of a bunch of gangsters sitting around in place of Jesus and the Apostles?"

Roger scoffed, and I looked at him. He squinted his eyes and crinkled his face into deep creases, shaking his head like I was an idiot.

Knapczyk took a long drag from his cigarette, held the smoke in his lungs before blowing out the cloud. "Because I'm Catholic," he said with a smile, and Roger howled with laughter.

◆ ◆ ◆

Knapczyk's wife looked tired when she got home from her job at the hospital. She was stocky and as tall as her husband, but with her shoulders sagging, bags hanging low under her eyes, she looked small and defeated.

When she walked into the dining room her eyes were half-closed, mouth pulled into a frown, but when she saw me sitting at the table her face lit up.

"Who's this?" she asked, walking over and placing her hands on my cheeks.

I smiled and tried to look pleased to see her, even though I was uncomfortable with women, especially older ones. My mother had never touched me the way Mrs. Knapczyk was holding my face.

"Let's get you something to eat, yeah?" she said, squeezing my wrist and pulling me toward the kitchen.

"Couldn't have any kids of our own," I heard Knapczyk shout to Roger as she pulled me out of the dining room. "So when she sees one, she gets all giddy."

Mrs. Knapczyk sat me at the kitchen table with a glass of milk, turned toward the stove, rummaging through cabinets, pulling out an assortment of ingredients and pots and pans.

"How old are you, Alex?" she asked with her back turned to me.

"Nine."

"Perfect," she said. "That's just perfect. I'm making you *chruściki*." She began pouring flour and eggs into a large mixing bowl. "My mother made these for me after my first Communion. Have you had your first Communion yet?"

She was now pouring cream into the bowl with one hand, digging through a cabinet with the other, pulling out a whisk.

"I don't think so." I had no idea what she was talking about.

"Oh. I'm sure your mom will have you do it soon. That's okay. We'll celebrate a little early. That's okay, right?" She turned and smiled a wide grin, eyes large and frantic.

"Sure," I said, sipping the glass of milk. Mrs. Knapczyk muttered to herself as she mixed the bowl, placing a pan on the stove and filling it with oil using her free hand. She moved with grace and precision, as if she'd been planning our meeting for weeks. I looked around the kitchen, at framed photos of nieces and nephews, pictures of her and Detective Knapczyk on their wedding day. They were young and thin and healthy. She smiled wide in the picture and Knapczyk stood expressionless, serious, like he was born police.

Above their wedding photos was an old painting of a bearded man, long hair hanging to his shoulders, a large gold medallion with a face hugging his chest. He was surrounded by a light blue sky, a single flame perched above his head like the wick of a candle.

"Is that Jesus?" I asked, and Mrs. Knapczyk turned to me with a look of surprise.

"Jesus? Oh, honey, no." She walked to the table, sat across from me and laid out her palms, signaling with her chin for me to place my hands on top of hers. "That's St. Jude," she said in low voice, almost a whisper. "You don't know St. Jude?"

I stared at her, anxiety bubbling.

"He's the patron saint of lost causes, impossible things. We pray to St. Jude for those who don't pray for themselves." She paused for a moment. "It's for Henry and all those he serves."

"Henry?"

"Yeah, Henry," she said, tapping the wedding photo, Detective Knapczyk's expressionless face. "Would you like to read the Bible with me sometime, Alex?"

"I...well..." I squirmed in my seat.

"That's enough, Mary," Detective Knapczyk was standing at the kitchen door. "We need some bonding time. Just the men," he smiled at his wife, and motioned for me to follow.

"Don't go too far," Mrs. Knapczyk called. "The *chruściki* will be done before you know it!"

Detective Knapczyk led me down the hallway, waddling silently except for the wheeze of his breath. We walked into his office, where Roger stood waiting, a windowless room lit by the bare bulb of a lamp sitting on a large oak desk and the static of a small television in the corner. There were flags for every Chicago team except the Cubs lining the walls.

"You really like oak," Roger said.

"Nothing like it," Knapczyk said, pounding the wood with his palm. "I want to show you two something," he wheeled himself in his chair over to the small television in the corner. He popped a tape in the VCR, and the static on the TV turned to a black-and-white image of a convenience store counter.

"Surveillance footage," Knapczyk said.

Roger and I stood and watched the screen.

The man behind the counter was in his fifties, balding, a white shirt buttoned to the collar.

"This is down on 63rd," Knapczyk said, raising his eyebrows as if that was saying something.

A few customers came to the counter, buying beer or cigarettes or paying for gas. A young man pushed through the entrance with his hood up.

"Watch this guy," Knapczyk said, tapping a fingernail over the hooded man on the screen.

A few minutes went by, and it looked like the store cleared out. The hooded man walked to the register, placed a tall can of beer on the counter. He pointed behind the clerk, motioning to the cigarettes he wanted. The clerk turned to fetch the pack.

"Watch his hands," Knapczyk said as the hooded man reached an arm around his back and pulled a pistol from his waistband, pointing it at the clerk. The clerk turned and raised his hands in the air, cigarettes clenched in his palm. It looked like the hooded man was shouting, motioning toward the register with the gun.

It took me a moment to see it was Knapczyk that burst through the entrance. He was plainclothes but he had his gun out, and before I knew it, he unloaded four or five shots into the hooded man, who fell to the ground, his torso landing outside the camera's view, his legs writhing in the frame. The clerk ducked behind the counter when the shots went off, and Knapczyk moved slowly toward the hooded man, his gun still drawn.

He pressed stop on the VCR.

"I wasn't even on duty," Knapczyk said, smiling, turning to me and Roger who stood in shock. My stomach felt like I'd swallowed gravel. "I was just there gassing up, saw it through the window and lit the fucker up."

He turned to me; a smile cocked on his face. Roger put his hand on my shoulder. The *chruściki* sizzled from the kitchen. It smelled foreign—

chaotic—salt and sugar and oil all mixed together. Nothing was right. Everything I knew about life and myself and family seemed to be replaced with the gravel, heavy and uncertain.

Roger squeezed my shoulder, and I looked at his smiling face. I loved him, envied him, wanted to be him in a few a short years—the way every boy feels about his father no matter how horrible of a man he really is—but I wouldn't know that, what the feeling meant, or how horrible he was. I wouldn't know for a long time.

◆ ◆ ◆

Roger didn't say much on the ride home. It was easy to stay silent, hide under the noise in his truck. The engine rumbled and the cracked muffler rattled, clutch grinding in first and third. My ears rung after long drives.

On the way to Halsted, we passed the Nativity of Our Lord, its steeple towering over the street. "It's one of the oldest churches in the city," Roger said, pointing, raising his voice above the engine.

"Is it Catholic?" I asked.

"It is," Roger nodded.

"Are we Catholic?"

Roger squirmed in his seat. "I am," he mumbled and stared out the windshield. He shifted and the transmission moaned.

"Do you know St. Jude?" I asked.

Roger looked at me and cracked a smile. "Yeah, I know St. Jude."

"He's the patron saint of lost causes and impossible things," I parroted Mrs. Knapczyk's words as well as I could remember.

"That's right," Roger said.

"Can we go to Mass on Sunday?"

Roger wrinkled his forehead. "I don't think we need to."

He turned on Halsted, back toward the North Side.

"Why did he shoot him?" I asked, and I could tell by the way Roger's face softened he was thinking of it too.

He stayed silent for a moment longer. "Because he's a lost cause," Roger said.

I looked out the window, watched the houses and porches fly by. The muffler squealed, Roger shifted, and I wondered who he meant. If the lost cause was the hooded man, or Detective Knapczyk. As I thought it over, I decided there was no point praying to St. Jude. I decided there were no lost causes, and after watching the man's legs writhe on the screen, there certainly were no impossible things.

Caravan

Really, Roger and I looked nothing alike. I knew it. I wasn't stupid. I must have been twelve when I started to notice Roger's blue eyes, the way he walked, swinging his long arms around his thin frame. Roger stood at least six-two and couldn't have weighed more than a buck sixty. I remember looking in the mirror hanging above the bathroom sink, brushing the thin hair from my eyes, staring at my deep brown irises. My mother's were a piercing green, under half-closed, sleepy blinks. I took off my shirt, grabbed the flab on my stomach, studying the cellulite that ran from my armpits to my hip.

"Isn't he supposed to thin out soon?" I heard Roger say from the living room. "I mean, he's got to hit puberty at some point."

My mother said nothing. All I heard was the ice clinking in her glass.

As I stared in the mirror, I thought if I had a mother who gave a shit, she would have called me a late-bloomer.

◆ ◆ ◆

My friend Tom and his family drove around in their family station wagon, oldies and shit blaring from the windows, Tom and his father actually singing the songs together like those redheads from that Partridge Family show Roger used to watch in the evenings.

I acted like all their family shit was corny. I needed them, though, Tom and his family. Roger had gone to work one morning and hadn't come home, had left without so much as a goodbye, and since then my mother hadn't gotten out of bed. I ate dinner at Tom's place every night, basically lived there on the weekends.

The last time I'd seen Roger was the night before he left. He poked his head in my door about one or two in the morning.

"Alex," he said in a whisper. "Alex, wake up."

I opened my eyes and saw the stale light of the kitchen pouring from behind him. "Huh?" I whined in a childish moan.

"You asleep?" he said.

I grunted again.

"I'll see you soon," he said, and I could sense him standing in the doorway for a long time. For a moment, I racked my sleep-addled brain for anything I'd done wrong that week or that month. I waited for a blow. He'd never come into my room like this before. I don't think he'd ever really been in my room at all. He'd always just shouted for me to come out if he needed something. But now he stayed with his head poking through the door for what felt like an eternity, whimpering. He inhaled through thick mucus, a tear zig-zagging between the wrinkles of his skin. It was strange and vulnerable, and I know I'll remember it for the rest of my life.

Roger didn't even take a bag with him the next day, and I found out a couple weeks after he was gone all his clothes were still hanging in the closet. They smelled like Marlboros and sun, cement smoothed with a trowel early in the morning. They smelled like when his mustache got long and curled into his mouth, and he complained about chewing on the hair during dinner, even though he never trimmed it. The dirt under his fingernails. Dark black crawling between his teeth.

I remember the flick of a cheap lighter, smoke creeping into my room. The carbonated sizzle of a beer poured into a tall glass and the sound of it tumbling down his throat, stubble dancing on his neck as he sucked it down.

◆ ◆ ◆

I knocked on my mother's bedroom door. "Mom," I yelled. She didn't answer. "The landlord stuck this under the door," I said, pushing the notice into her room. It wasn't an eviction notice. Not yet, at least. It was just a threat, a *we're going to kick you the fuck out if you don't pay but haven't done shit yet* notice.

We'd been evicted before, long ago when Roger was still in the navy. I knew they needed to have an official document from Cook County, not just some hand-written *fuck you, pay me* piece of paper from the landlord pushed under the door.

A couple days later, she finally came out. Her blond hair was matted, makeup smeared on her face. She walked to the counter to fix a drink.

"I know he left," I said. "But is Dad coming back?" It took me a moment to notice I said it, that I didn't call him Roger. I felt embarrassed, a sharp emptiness in my gut.

My mother stirred the screwdriver with her finger, sucking the liquid from her paint-chipped nail. "He's not actually your father," she said, and walked back to her room, ice cubes clinking against the glass.

I didn't say a word. It didn't matter what she said. It didn't matter Roger had left. I knew he was coming back, that eventually we would all be together again.

◆ ◆ ◆

"Maybe he's dead," I asked my mother when she finally started coming out of her room again.

"We'd have gotten his truck back," she said, brushing her hair from her eyes. "The cops would have come."

"Maybe they took it with them," I said.

"Who?" my mother scoffed.

I'd been imagining Roger held hostage or killed in a fight, or maybe he'd had a few too many after work and twisted his truck around a pole in Portage Park. I would never tell my mother these things, so all I said was "Whoever he's with."

My mother laughed and walked back to her bedroom, clicked the radio on. The muffled voice of

John Prine's "Caravan of Fools" carried through her old wooden door. And I swore he was singing to me.

Rat King

I sat on Tom's parent's bed, refinished hardwood under my toes, watching Scottie Pippen shoot free throws. The camera cut to under the hoop, a straight view of the game from courtside seats. I squinted; rubbed my eyes. The world looked like it was wrapped in cellophane.

Tom and Javier were on mushrooms, more of a body high, all stretched out. They said each step felt like it moved halfway across the room.

They ate both bags without me, washed the foul taste down with glasses of orange juice. When I saw their dilated pupils, the black circle carpeting Tom's blue iris, I threw a tantrum, like any left-out thirteen-year-old.

I stormed off to Tom's parents' bedroom, and about thirty minutes later, Tom walked through the door holding a plastic bag with a single square of paper in the middle.

"I feel bad, Alex," he said.

"Yeah, we were all supposed to try this together," I said.

"Here. Take this." He handed me the bag with the square paper inside.

"What is it?"

"It's a dose," he said, his jaw working in a loop as he spoke. "If you want, you can trip with us."

He had dug the hit of acid out of the back of a drawer in his bedroom. It was at least a year old, and he wasn't sure if it would still work. I took the bag and placed the paper on my tongue.

"Don't swallow," Tom said. "Suck on it until it dissolves." He walked back to his bedroom. Twenty minutes later, Scottie Pippen was shooting free throws, and the hardwood court crawled over his high-tops.

Tom and Javier were going to Lakeview High in the fall, and I was stuck at Edgewater Elementary. I could hear them laughing from Tom's bedroom, shooting a rubber ball through a hoop hanging on the back of his door. I wanted to laugh and shoot hoops with them, but I was stuck to the bed, staring at Scottie Pippen, beads of sweat not running down his skin but dancing across his face, crawling like a colony of maggots under his skin, burrowing in and out as he set picks and sunk layups.

It was just me and Scottie, who looked like a hologram on the screen, princess Leia projected from R2-D2: *You're my only hope*.

The door burst open. I jumped, hands shaking. Tom and Javier stood in the doorway, inviting smiles spreading across their faces.

"You okay?" Tom asked.

"Yes," I said in a soft squeal.

"Damn, Alex's flyin'," Javier said, his smile bigger, exposing a missing front tooth. As far as I knew, he had never had a full set.

"We gotta go. My parents are coming back from the movie soon," Tom said. "We're going to Javier's house."

"Nobody's home?" I asked.

Javier chuckled. "My parents are nice. You don't need to worry about them."

We walked on Belmont toward Sheffield, on our way to the Red Line. Movement was effortless, cars rolling slow, faces on foot traffic loving. Tom bought us each tall cans of iced tea from the liquor store on the corner before we got to the train.

A white guy on his bike blew the red light in front of us as we waited for the sign to flash *Walk*. He was moving fast, hair trailing out of his helmet, fluttering in the wind.

At first, I wasn't sure if I imagined it. The screeching of the tires sounded familiar, like it could have been in my head. But the thump of his body, the slap of his skin against the taxi, was too foreign to be made up. Someone screamed. It was real. I was sure of it.

His bike was lying bent in the intersection. The driver rushed out of the Yellow Cab, flipped to his stomach, peering under the car. I squatted to my ankles, ass almost brushing the sidewalk. The still dusk provided just enough light to see the biker's lump trapped, crumpled in a ball under the taxi's chassis.

I walked into the street toward the cab. Tom turned to Javier, asking what I was doing.

"Alex," he yelled, his voice cracking. "Alex, get the fuck back here."

I grabbed the cab's wheel well and pulled. I knew I could lift it, maybe just enough for him to slide out and he'd jump back on his bike and ride away. I pulled until I heard sirens from the ambulance, and the driver rose from his belly on the street, looked at me trying to lift his cab, and with a quick swing backhanded me, his hand heavy, the hair of his knuckles rough on my soft face.

"Fuck off, kid," he said through a choppy accent, bits of Arabic or Farsi singing softly after.

I fell to the asphalt, sat for a moment in bewilderment. When I looked over my shoulder, Tom's eyes were wide, frightened; he was shaking his head. Javier stood motionless, sipping from his iced tea, an indifferent look on his face.

Tom set his tea on the cement and walked back on Belmont toward his parents' house. Javier motioned for me to follow him. I stood up as the ambulance came, a crowd forming around the scene. I looked between Tom walking back home and Javier moving toward the train. I only had a moment to decide.

We ran up the stairs and jumped on the Howard train just as the doors were closing. We didn't say a word until we got to Javier's place in Uptown.

When we walked in, his parents were playing cards at the kitchen table. Two little kids slept on couches in the living room. We walked to his bedroom, the rest of the night spent playing video games in an old lamp's dim light. When I finally fell asleep on the carpet next to his bed, the sun poking through the curtains, I dreamed I lifted the cab, pushed it upside down. The man was free, but he didn't get up. He stayed in a pile on the street.

I didn't see Tom much after that, after he went off to high school. Javier I saw in Uptown every day. I started skipping class to hang out with him in the neighborhood. By the end of ninth grade, he had been kicked out of school and was covered in tattoos, mostly of common street vermin. He had a pigeon on his forearm, roach on his calf, and a rat on his chest, climbing up his neck. By the next summer nobody called him Javier anymore. He was Rat King.

◆ ◆ ◆

Michael Jordan's tongue stuck out every time he drove to the hoop. Not like a schoolboy teasing the new kid in the cafeteria, but flat on his chin, jaws stretched open like he was sitting in a dentist's chair.

In the spring of ninth grade, me and Javier played basketball at Buttercup Park every day after lunch, skipping our afternoon classes to perfect a finger roll. I wore my Jordan jersey every afternoon, slipped it over a white t-shirt, and splashed my New Balances through the puddles to sink jump shots. I knew Javier wouldn't go near the puddles in his Pumps. Any time his ankle rolled and the toe of his high-top skidded over the court's cracked cement, he'd try and call a time out, sit on the benches and sigh and mutter about the scuff on his shoe. "C'mon. They're just fucking sneakers," I'd whine until he laced back up, pumped the rubber basketball on the shoe's tongue—which he swore gave him at least two extra inches on his jump—and got back in the game.

I drove to the hoop, ran my thin shoulder into Javier's muscle, stretched my jaw open as wide as I could, slapping my tongue on the soft skin of my chin, and brought my arm up for a layup. Javier stuffed it, slapping the ball with enough force to knock it into the damp grass.

"Ooohh shit!" he cried, sliding his feet against the ground to do a little Harlem Shake in victory. I stomped through the spring mud to get the ball, my jersey spotted with dirt and stains from lunch.

I came back to the court, dribbled a few times, faked a drive, Javier spreading his arms out, swatting at the ball, but before I could get the shot off a whistle blew, a two-finger high-pitched sound normally reserved for parents calling their kids for dinner or an elementary teacher whipping an unruly classroom back into shape. The type of whistle that still straightened our spines.

We looked to the benches that faced Sheridan, where the guys from the homeless shelters that littered the neighborhood spent most of their day.

"Young man," one of the men called, pulling two calloused fingers from his mouth, motioning to Javier. I recognized the man from outside Preston Bradley, a landmark six-story former church and theater turned into transitional housing. The man calling to Javier was always draped in donated clothes, sitting on a bench in front of the building, sucking on a cigarette, low grumbles under his breath directed at no one in particular.

Javier lifted his hands up, a quick shrug.

"C'mere, kid," the man said. "I got a job for you."

Javier jogged over, his basketball shorts fluttering behind him. The roach had already been scratched into his calf, pigeon etched on his forearm, but the rat on his neck wouldn't come for another couple months.

The two talked for a few minutes, the man running a hand through his tangled curls, "Goddamn, kid. Two dollars is all I'll give you," he said, Javier shaking his head, arguing about something.

"Fine," the man finally agreed, handing Javier some bills. Javier took off down a side street, toward Kenmore where the CVL teenagers hung out on the porch of one of their grandma's split-level's all day. He wasn't gone long, and while the man waited, he chatted with the others, sipping High Life.

When Javier came back, he dropped something in the man's hand, and we walked the few blocks back to his parents' apartment. We sat in the living room, Javier pulling a corner bag from his pocket, breaking it open on the glass coffee table.

"Old prick tried to give me two dollars," he said, exposing the hole in his jaw. "He owes those kids money for dope, so he thinks he can just get one of us to get his shit for him and they won't know any better."

I thought about him saying "one of us" like it was me and him together. I wasn't just tagging along.

He chopped his school ID through the powder with his head down, separated it into lines, and pushed it into a spoon he got from the kitchen. He pulled out what I thought was a pen, but when he popped off the bright orange cap a needle shined in the sun. He poured a little water into the spoon and cooked the shot, sucking the brown mixture into the needle through the filter of a cigarette he'd ripped open.

"Try this," he said with a smile. He knelt next to me, told me to close my eyes and pump my fist. I could feel the warm liquid mixing with my blood. I leaned back, kept my eyes closed. My nose started itching, jaw didn't quite seem to fit in my mouth anymore. When I opened my eyes, the world was choppy, all mixed up. Javier was leaning his head back on a recliner, eyes closed.

I gagged a few times but got ahold of myself. My body felt like it had just woken from a deep sleep, skin clammy and red like I just got out of a hot shower. I picked up a half-smoked cigarette from his parents' ashtray on the coffee table, lit it, and let the smoke flow from my mouth. Javier's head jerked up, and his eyes closed again. He curled in the chair, elbows hugging his abdomen, wrists and fingers bent awkwardly like his hands were broken. For a moment, he looked just like the biker trapped under the cab, limbs tied in a knot. As I stared at him, noticing the shape of his chest and a mustache poking from his lip, I thought he wouldn't be the Javier I knew much longer.

◆ ◆ ◆

Javier got the rat tattooed on his neck by Micky's brother. I don't know if Micky was his real name, but that's what everyone called him. Micky was always hanging around the neighborhood, selling CDs on the corners, or trying to trade them for a shot.

"I bet my brother would do it for a hundred fifty," Micky said, pushing long strands of thin blond hair out of his eyes as a cigarette burned between his knuckles.

I never liked Micky. There was something about his bright green eyes and banana-yellow teeth that creeped me out. He was sickly skinny, face sucked in, cheekbones like they could cut glass.

"What else has he done?" Javier asked.

"All sorts of shit," Micky said. "He's got a shop on Howard."

Javier thought it over. "Hundred fifty is a lot."

"This shit is permanent," Micky said, raising his thin arms out, exposing tracks running across his veins. "You need somebody who's gonna do it right. I'm telling you. Here, look," Micky stuck the cigarette in his mouth, turned to the side and lifted the t-shirt covering his thin frame. On his ribcage, amid freckles and beauty marks and the pink scar on his lower abdomen where his appendix was removed, was a perfectly tattooed pin-up girl. She sat with her legs crossed, garters riding up her thighs. Both arms resting behind her head, eyes closed, chest pushed out, mouth puckered, waiting for a kiss on her bright red lips. Javier looked down at the crudely done pigeon on his forearm. It looked like it was drawn in pen compared to Micky's tattoo.

"Hundred fifty will work," Javier said. "We'll come by tomorrow."

"I'll let him know," Micky said, and walked down the block toward the lake.

"How're you gonna get a hundred fifty bucks?" I asked Javier.

"Don't worry about it. C'mon," Javier said, leading me toward the train.

We rode the Red Line down to Belmont. I stared at the corner of Sheffield where we'd seen the biker get hit just a year or so earlier. I'd dreamed about the accident again the night before.

Javier led me to an old greystone. It was the same two-flat where I had dropped acid for the first time.

"Why are we at Tom's place?" I asked. "I haven't seen him in like a year."

"Because he's the richest guy I know," Javier said, hopping the fence into the grass, walking around to the back of the house. We'd both been there a thousand times. We knew the back door was old, not flimsy, but much easier for Javier to break open with just a few thrusts of his shoulder.

When we walked in the smell hit me. I remembered spending weekends in the kitchen, Friday and Saturday afternoons watching TV and action movies in the living room. Tom still had the same basketball hoop stuck on his door.

We walked down the hall to his parents' room, the walls still covered in Tom's baby pictures. Javier started digging through everything, tipping over jewelry boxes, pocketing anything that seemed valuable.

"Here," he said, handing me a gold watch he found in a bedside table before going to rummage through a chest of drawers across the room. I shoved the watch in my pocket.

"Got it," Javier said, pulling a wad of cash from Tom's father's sock drawer. I thought it was probably two or three hundred. I looked around the room. The mattress was flipped, everything dumped on the floor. The place was destroyed.

"Let's get out of here," Javier said.

As we walked toward the stairs, pockets overflowing, there was a banging on the front door, three loud thumps. I thought my heart was going to jump out of my chest.

"Shit," I said, running back to the bedroom, peaking out the window. A squad car and a couple elderly neighbors stood out front.

"Hello," echoed from downstairs. It sounded like it was coming from the back door, the gruff voice of an overfed cop. I looked for Javier, who was already out the window on the front balcony, leaping to the soft grass below.

"He's here! He's here!" the neighbors yelled. Out the window, I saw Javier bolting down the street, wad of cash still gripped in his hand. Before I could get out on the balcony, the officer's hairy knuckles met the back of my head, sending me down to the hardwood. He cuffed my hands and led me downstairs. I was dizzy from the punch. I could barely walk. He pushed me in the back of his car, Tom and his parents driving up in the family's station wagon just as he shut the door. They spoke with the officer who hit me, who handed his father the gold watch from my pocket.

The family stood with disgusted looks slapped across their faces, arms folded, shaking their heads. I imagined Tom's mother saying things like *Where did he go wrong. He used to be such a nice boy.* Tom and his father stared at me with blood in their eyes. They all stood together, a unit, just like a family.

◆ ◆ ◆

My mother didn't show up to get me from the police station until the next morning.

"She must be running late," I told the officer in booking.

"She's got twelve hours before I have to call DCFS," he said, and I laid down on the bench and waited for whatever would happen next.

I dreamed of the accident. I moved the car, picked it up and flipped it on its roof, the metal crunching as it turned. The driver was pissed.

Tom ran off, sprinting down the block, jumping in a station wagon driven by his parents. His father sat in the driver's seat, shaking his head, a look of disgust on his face. When the station wagon drove away, the tires squealed, and I remembered the man lying in the street. As I looked down, his hair turned from long brown locks to a high-top fade, long limbs twisted in a knot: Scottie Pippen, with maggots on his face burrowing in and out under his skin. Javier walked over, handed me his can of iced tea, bending down and kissing Scottie Pippen on the forehead, running a palm over his eyes so they closed.

He walked to the fallen bike and picked it up. I sat on the handlebars and we rode through the neighborhood to Uptown, to a lemonade stand on Broadway and Wilson. The man at the stand smiled gold teeth, handed Javier a fresh rig and a gram. We went to his parents' house to shoot up in the living room. His mother was screaming at his father in the kitchen, saying he cheated her in dominos.

When the needle pushed in my arm blood shot into the rig. I pushed the plunger, but before the shot entered my bloodstream, the needle broke. Javier's eyes grew with fear. I grabbed my bicep above the vein. Javier told me the needle would flow through my blood and get to my heart. If it did, I'd die. He took off his belt and wrapped it like a tourniquet around my arm, and we rode to an emergency room on the bike.

The nurses and doctors and orderlies at the hospital all looked me up and down, the same look of disgust Tom's family had when I sat in the back of the squad car. The hospital staff shook their heads, waved a hand, turning me away. As Javier led me out of the emergency room, I looked back one more time to plead for help.

"You're on your own," they said. "You're on your own."

Heartbeat

The guard showed me around my first day. When I walked on the unit, the first person I saw was Jon standing shirtless in front of his room, shouting *Enter* in a pubescent voice still searching for its manhood. All one hundred twenty pounds of him waited for the electronic buzz of the lock so he could go inside.

My head nodded at the guard's instructions, eyes scanning the kitchen-table tattoo of a feather running down Jon's left ribcage and *Harper*, which I found out was his last name, scrawled in Old English letters with what looked like mimeo ink.

Jon turned back to look, his nose crooked and mangled, like it had grown that way. His eyes were a bit too close on a lopsided skull. I thought he must have been dropped as a baby. A smooth philtrum and thin vermilion (words I'd only learn later), undoubtedly from prenatal alcohol exposure.

I wondered when he first noticed it, or if he ever did? If he knew how his face looked? His eyes, nose, mouth spread out like a drunk slapped it on after trying to sleep it off, before the morning's first swig.

He mouthed something at me before entering his cell. I couldn't quite make out what he said but I didn't think it was friendly.

Jon sneered through the square observation window on the door. He banged against the metal once the lock thumped. Before I knew it, all the windows had faces and eyes peering through. They all started banging, voices pushing through the cracks in the door, asking if I had money on my books, what I was there for. One asked if I was a virgin.

We made it to the last cell at the end of the hall. The officer's station was at least fifty feet away from my door.

My new home was bigger than expected, carpeted, two beat-up wooden dressers for clothes, two metal bed frames, one with a mattress.

I hadn't been afraid when the sheriff shackled my hands and ankles, pushing my thin frame onto the plastic seat in the back of the car, driving a few hundred miles away from home. I didn't consider what it would be like, or that I would actually end up here. But standing in my room, listening to the endless banging and shouting outside, my knees shook. The loudest pounding came from my chest. I wept for the first time in years.

I made my bed and laid down, thanking God I was in a cell by myself, waiting to go to lunch in a few hours.

◆ ◆ ◆

I want tattoos like yours, meaningful, tough, fading from long hours of hard work. I'm not sure what I'd get yet, but I'm working on it. I spend most of my time here sketching stuff, ideas. If I was brave like you, I would have joined the navy, or the army, got to work. I'm not. I wish I was.

I don't want child support, even though I know Mom is coming after you. She told me you aren't my real father. I'll stick up for you if she takes you to court. Last time I knew she was in the shelter, Cornerstone, I think. That one on Leland. I hope she gets a new place by the time I get out of here.

I don't care if you're not really my dad. I don't need your money. When I got caught up, I saw my old friend Tom standing outside with his family. You might remember him, the short kid with long bangs and green eyes. He used to steal Camels from your jacket (back when you smoked straights), and we'd sneak out to the trees at the elementary school, take a couple puffs, and bury them in the dirt. I know you never liked him. You called his dad a pussy. But he's really not so bad when you get to know him.

I saw them all together and it reminded me of us. Remember that time you took everyone to Montrose Beach, and you drank High Life and laid out in the sand? Mom forgot to bring the towels, so when we took the bus home, we were all soaked, sand sticking all over our skin. You kept saying how embarrassed you were.

If you write back, we can talk about how to deal with Mom. You know her, she won't stop until she gets what she wants from you. She's just like that.

◆ ◆ ◆

I fell asleep about an hour after I got in my cell. I woke to chatter and doors slamming, a kid holding my door open with one arm, making sure not to cross the line into my room.

"Lunch time," he said, motioning for me to follow him downstairs to the cafeteria with the rest of the unit. "I'm Lars," he told me as we lined up with the rest of the group. "Your trustee. I'll be your buddy for the first week, make sure you don't get too fucked up before you even get settled."

Lars told me he was from downstate. He definitely had that country look, short and stocky with a shaved head. He came from a long line of hay balers and his forearms showed it. He had *Thug Life* tattooed on his massive wrists.

"They put some money on my books for these jobs. Once you're here for a few months you can do it too."

We sat at a table near the windows overlooking the basketball court, eating chicken nuggets. Jon strolled by in ankle-length shorts and a hoody with the sleeves cutoff, so everyone could see his tattoos. He got his tray and sat at a table adjacent to Lars and me.

"These fucking guys," Lars said, motioning to Jon's table. "They talk too slowly and smell like shit and fight at any chance they can get. Stay away from them."

I sat nervously, eyes darting from Lars to the two Native inmates only a few feet away. It wasn't until Lars said *Savage* that I noticed a perk in Jon's head. He twitched a little, the lumpy skull bobbing on a skinny neck.

Jon stood and walked to the cafeteria counter, asking the cook for a new metal fork because he dropped his. He strolled back, Jordans thumping against the cement tile. For a second, I thought he was going to pass us.

His eyes were pointed to the floor when he sprung at Lars, leaping over the table, stretching out his thin frame for distance. The fork glimmered under the fluorescent light as he thrust it into Lars's chest.

In Jon's haste he'd held the fork wrong, upside-down with the prongs angled towards the floor; the utensil bent in half against Lars's breast bone. It was still enough force to knock the country boy backward in his chair, even if it didn't puncture the skin.

For a moment, Jon stood over Lars studying the bent fork, trying to piece together how the assault went wrong. He gained his composure, bringing a heavy foot down on Lars's neck before the staff tackled him and dragged him back to his room.

Lars was moved to a new unit on the same floor of the building, just across the hall from ours. Jon had to stay in his room the rest of the night.

The other inmates whispered about the fight, their game of telephone becoming more imaginative as time passed. Finally, before lights out, I heard Lars was on the brink of death from the fork puncturing his lung.

They never assigned me a new trustee.

◆ ◆ ◆

Sometimes people have to leave. Save themselves, right? It doesn't mean they don't give a shit. They need to take care of themselves. Maybe I'm just learning that the hard way.

The court proceeding was quick. Mom signed some documents waving parental rights and the judge gave me six months in juvie.

I jumped on the deal.

Javier doesn't write me, neither does anyone else from back home. Mom must be sober, or she's trying to get me to go along with all the child support stuff, because she's been sending a card every month, usually with a picture of a butterfly or flowers on the front. They always have short messages about the weather, how much rain she had or what the forecast looks like that week.

One card said she'd talked to you, that you moved all the way out to California, and you asked about me. I ask the desk everyday if anything came from San Bernardino, anywhere in California. But they only shake their heads.

A few days after I sent you the first letter, it came back with a big "Return to Sender" stamp over your name. The San Bernardino address was where mom said you lived.

It doesn't matter. I'll keep writing. Hoping maybe one day, an envelope will come back addressed to me.

◆ ◆ ◆

A couple weeks after the incident with Lars, the place was starting to fill up. They told me I was getting a roommate. Jon walked into my room carrying his mattress, placed it on the metal bedframe in the opposite corner from me, and began organizing his belongings on the scuffed wooden dresser in silence.

He spent most of his time quiet, focused. I wasn't sure if he'd always been that way or if it was the pile of medication they delivered to our room every morning.

He kept his head down, carefully designing tattoos he planned to get when he went home. He wrote everything carefully, slowly, in bold Old English lettering. He didn't see a point writing any other way.

His creations were plastered on the walls of our room. A couple nights after he moved in, I asked him what they meant, what he was trying to create with tattoo designs and lettering.

Folks, was all he'd tell me.

I noticed the pointed stars he etched into his desk in the classroom downstairs, how he attacked all the new kids coming in that talked about *People,* but I wasn't sure how deep in the life he was.

He was in a gang, that was certain, but I still only believed about half of the stories he told me.

"I ran a hundred pounds of meth from the reservation to Omaha," he said one night, before I let him know he was full of shit and he started giggling like he was getting away with something.

When he was serious, he'd focus intently on a single spot on the wall while he was talking, not making eye contact while the words unspooled from his mouth like a ball rolling into traffic.

As the weeks went on, I started helping him design tattoos. I'd give him three words and he'd draw it up. Something like *razorblade, cross, Mercedes* and he'd come back the next night with a smug look on his face, proud to hand me the sketch.

"I told you I can do anything. Give me something harder next time," he'd tell me before getting into his bunk.

Eventually, we started talking about where we grew up.

"Yeah, I get it," he'd say when I talked about the apartment I lived in with my mother. "I lived with my mom and grandma. I haven't seen them in a year or so."

He'd get jealous when the cards came from my mother, stop talking to me for a few hours, but by lights-out we were always on good terms again.

One-night Jon showed me his stash of Adderall. He had been cheeking the medication every morning and stashing it in a hole he carved in the wood behind the dresser. One of us kept watch while the other opened capsules and crushed the timed-release balls into a snortable powder.

We each had a few lines, blowing them up our nostrils with animated vigor, tilting our heads back, waiting for the drip.

Paranoia set in as the amphetamine ran through our blood. We got into our bunks so when the officer came to shine a flashlight into the room they'd think we were asleep.

We were lying silent for a time, Jon's eyes wide, palms sweating; he began to chatter about his life on the reservation, back in South Dakota. "Things got bad after some shit with Octavio."

I stayed silent.

"Octavio wasn't even full Sioux," Jon said, his mouth running faster than I'd ever seen. "His dad was Mexican, lived in Sioux Falls. He stayed on the reservation with his grandma, who was Yankton.

"Octavio was short and stocky, a couple grades older than me. He had a rosary tattooed on the top of his hand, the beads coming down his wrist." Jon held up his arm and traced a V-shape down toward his fingers. "Cross right here on the knuckle." He lifted his middle finger in the air.

"Octavio gave me the feather," Jon said, patting his ribcage under the blanket. "When I was thirteen. We loved each other." He told me about going to Octavio's grandmother's house after school to eat dried deer and turkey, spending Saturdays smoking cigarettes in a wooded area near their home.

"It all happened when I was thirteen, right after the feather. We stole this jug of Gallo from my grandma, went out to the woods."

I imagined Jon and Octavio tromping through the trees, the cherry of their cigarettes bobbing in the darkness as the night wrapped around them.

"We got through half the bottle, but that shit creeps up on you. Before we knew it, we had no clue where we were, this place we'd been to a thousand times. We knew we weren't making it back before the sun came up. Luckily, we had lighters so we could get a fire going."

I thought of the boys' smiling red teeth as a fire surged, a chill running through the fall breeze.

"We were just sitting there, quiet, like we ran out of things to talk about. But then Octavio started in about his dad. He sounded different, though. His voice was higher, like his throat shrunk or something."

"Octavio started going on about how his dad wasn't shit, some loser mechanic who stole copper from the scrap yard behind the shop. Octavio's eyes started getting all red when he was talking. He kept saying he couldn't turn out to be the same person."

"I sat next to him when he really started blubbering. He was my friend, I hated seeing him like that. I could feel him shaking, but I couldn't tell if he was cold or what. I held my ear to his chest, listening to his heart beat, trying to see how fast it was going. I don't know if it was the wine, but his heart had a rhythm, it was moving faster and slower to a beat, like a drum was pumping his veins."

"When I came back up, he was just staring at me. He placed his lips to my mouth."

Jon stayed silent for a while. I thought he was done talking, but he started up again.

"We woke up with the sun, the dirt was cold, fire still smoldering. We didn't say anything as we walked back, and I didn't talk to him for a week. But I missed him, you know? I missed all the time we used to spend together. I caught him in the cafeteria at school and told him it was all right, that we could still be friends, maybe something else."

"He couldn't get it together, though, he started hugging me every time we saw each other, brushing the hair behind my ear. I heard some rumors about him, about us, from people at school and around the grocery. A couple weeks later his mom sent him to Sioux Falls to live with his dad."

Jon stopped talking at that point. We laid in bed, silent, I thought he might start back up again, but he rolled over. We were both still wired. I knew he wasn't sleeping.

◆ ◆ ◆

I remember the fancy dinners we used to go to every year for your birthday.

You'd eat the steak almost raw, mixing the mashed potatoes with the pool of blood left on the plate after the meat was gone.

After your fourth Maker's Mark, you'd order crème brulee for dessert. The server would carry out the little ceramic bowls on a platter, set one in front of each of us, pouring a small cup of sugar on top. They'd pull out a little blowtorch and melt the sugar at the table.

You'd tell me to sit back when the torch came out, but I loved the smell of burnt sugar and butane.

Mom would drive home in the middle of winter, the radio playing, your cigarette held to the window, all of us singing oldies at the top of our lungs. I guess you don't have to drive in snow anymore.

◆ ◆ ◆

My mother sent me her usual letter a month before my release. It was in a plain white envelope with an Elvis stamp and no return address.

There wasn't a card this time, just a single piece of lined paper, her cursive scratched across the page.

The facility had called her, trying to setup a plan for my "reentry," asking her questions about who lived in the house, her job, how much she drank and what drugs she used.

Her handwriting became sloppier as the letter went on.

She said she was sorry, that I couldn't come home, that she didn't think it was a good idea for me come back to the city at all.

A social worker came a few days after her letter arrived, asking if I had any relatives to stay with, where I'd like to move if they found a bed in a halfway house.

"You can live with me," Jon said after I read him the letter from Mom, telling him about the halfway house. "I'm going back out there. My grandma has some space in the basement. I'll even give you your first tattoo. All you have to do is find a place for six months until I get out."

I agreed, both of us knowing that once I found a place, we'd never see each other again.

At night we started talking about life after our release, what it would be like when I moved into the basement.

"My grandma makes stuffed trout every Saturday. We can camp out in the woods. Oh, shit, I came up with this, too." He handed me a sketch of two revolvers arched above a heart. But it wasn't a Valentine's Day heart, it was the real human organ. There were four valves, and arteries that connected to the muscle.

"I'll fix it up before I actually put it on you," he said.

A few weeks after my mother sent the letter, the social worker came back, saying they found me a place in a halfway house back in Chicago. It had been six months since I was home.

I packed my things the last night. Jon sat silently on his bed. I sat next to him, draping an arm over his thin shoulders.

He held his ear to my chest, listening to the rhythm.

Harbor

There was always touch. Maybe he didn't notice it the same way I did. He used to flex when I guarded him in one-on-one, at Buttercup Park when no one else was around. He had no reservations changing in front of me when we went to Montrose Beach. We never went to the bathrooms to change; they were always too crowded, and Javier said, the bushes were cleaner, anyway. Amidst the shrubs off the harbor, as deep as we could go in the short trail only a few feet from picnics and laughter and the smell of charcoal grills, he showed me his body. Every summer, we watched each other develop from grade-school peach fuzz to toned muscles and a forest of hair.

There were the nights, too. Most Saturdays his parents hosted their friends for late night games of brisca or dominos, round after round of hands slapping on the cheap wooden table, and after the laughing and drinking died down, the smell of fried plantains would linger in the small apartment, and he'd come off his bed and lay with me on the floor, breath hot and soft on my neck, and we held each other until the pigeons cooed at sunrise.

◆ ◆ ◆

I was staying at a halfway house: Trinity, on the West Side. My mother moved into a studio apartment on Magnolia and Ainslie. She started calling drunk in the middle of the day.

"This guy downstairs," she said, voice low and gruff like she just rolled out of bed, pushing through the static of the house phone. "Probably a guy, because his music is all loud bass and girls singing chorus. Anyway, he plays the same songs on repeat from nine to five like it's his job."

"Maybe you need to get out a little," I said. "We could meet and walk by the lake. You used to like going to the harbor when I was a kid." We were silent for a moment and I could almost hear her roll her eyes. "Have you talked to Roger?" I finally said.

"God knows where he is. I pray for him every night."

I could hear her hands moving behind the receiver, a quick sign of the cross. "I guess we just weren't enough for him."

I cringed when she talked about "us" like we had something other than day-drunk phone calls.

"Remember that time we all went to Six Flags together?"

She laughed. "Yeah, you ate three snow cones and threw up all over your shirt. Everybody stared like I was the worst mother."

"So you bought me a shirt from the gift shop. I changed in the bathroom and Roger bought us more snow cones. You were so mad." We laughed, and for a moment everything was good.

"He'll come back," she said. "He always does."

◆ ◆ ◆

Trinity House was overcrowded. They crammed everyone who'd been there less than a month in what they called "the ten-man room." Teenage boys on top of each other in bunk beds in the basement. The newest guys slept on the top bunks, bodies less than a foot from the ceiling. I laid on the plastic mattress under the word "Peckerwood" scratched in pencil on white paint now stained yellow from years of being spattered by various fluids.

Trinity was understaffed. Ms. Rebecca ran the place during the day, greeting us at breakfast every morning--smiling wide--a sweater or shawl hugging her body. Her hair and makeup were crafted every day with care, nails perfectly manicured with a flawless no-chip. There were other staff during the day, often students or interns working toward a master's degree, but they didn't last long. And as the sun set and lights-out approached, second shift ending, they all cleared out. There was always somebody at the front desk, twenty-four hours a day, to keep general tabs when kids came and went, but the ten-man room pretty much governed itself.

Two boys ran Trinity after second shift ended. Francis was tall and muscular, the kind of fifteen-year-old who never got carded for cigarettes or liquor. He was deep South Side Irish, Beverly or Morgan Park, nice family neighborhoods, really. He was arrested with a group of his friends after luring a black kid from their school to a park and trying to lynch him. Dominic was a rat-faced thief from Taylor Street whose grandparents somehow managed to hold on to their greystone after UIC spread through Little Italy. He said he lived in the three-flat with his parents and ten brothers and sisters. From the sound of it, the aldermen had been scheming ways to drive his family out of the 22nd Ward for generations, but they stuck in the greystone like mold.

"Wanna trade your slippers?" Francis said to a blond-haired kid who'd just came in that day, who was changing from his jeans into basketball shorts before bed. The boy was tall and thin, and looked like he was from Gold Coast or Old Town. Francis held up his months-old white slippers that were now turning gray.

"I'm good," the blond-haired boy said sheepishly. He was in way over his head.

Francis snatched the kid's new flip-flops, still wrapped in plastic, and tossed him the gray slippers. And while the two were talking, Dominic crept up behind and slid the new guy's jeans off the top bunk, emptied the pockets and had the money out of his wallet before the kid even noticed.

He had to know it was gone at some point. But he never said a thing. From then on, the boy didn't watch TV with the others or play basketball in the parking lot out back. He stayed on his bunk, only coming down to go to the bathroom when nobody else was around. That's just how it was.

◆ ◆ ◆

I circled Truman College looking for Javier, paced from Montrose to Foster, rode from Berwyn to

Sheridan, got off the train and walked back. Sometimes, I walked by my mother's building, but I never went up.

Every person who carried a basketball or lit a cigarette or wore white Reeboks had Javier's face, and for a moment, when I looked into their eyes, I saw him staring back at me. But I got a few steps closer and their faces turned back to a clerk at the liquor store, or a woman buying fruit, or a different boy on a different corner. It didn't really matter who they were. All I knew is they weren't him.

Micky stood on the corner, his yellow teeth and long nails posted up on Clarendon and Sunnyside, bouncing a yo-yo up and down. The plastic disc fell, nearly hitting the cracked cement, spun for moment, and with a slight flick climbed back to Micky's hand.

When he saw me, his eyes half-closed, a smirk poking from his thin lips, it was like he was looking through me, a faceless child on the street.

"Alex," he said, and the halitosis burned my nostrils. "Been awhile." He spun the yo-yo back toward the street.

"Yeah," I said, taking a step back. "Where'd you get that?"

"I found it in a can by the Aragon," he said, and he perked up, as if he'd been waiting all day for someone to ask him where he'd scored such a prize.

"You're pretty good," I said.

He tried walking the dog again but the plastic disc nicked the cement and stopped its spinning and lay lifeless on the sidewalk. He frowned.

"You know, I saw your mom the other day. She said you were back. Back in the city, at least."

"Where'd you see her?"

"At Rayan's, buying gin. She looked good," he said with a chuckle, wrapping the string again around the stem.

I stared at his thin face. I thought I could drag him across to Margate Park and drop a rock on his head. His skull would crack like a cheap vase.

"Relax," he said, smiling. "She doesn't look any worse than my mom. And my mom's all the way up on Howard. They got real corners there."

"What are you doing around here then?" I asked. "Why not stay up there?"

Micky shrugged his shoulders. "Sometimes," he said, puffing his chest and raising his arms like a bird, "you just got to spread your wings." He giggled and itched the side of his nose, from the looks of it his favorite spot. His skin was red and a large scab was forming. It bled a bit where he dragged a nail.

"You seen Javier?" I was getting annoyed with the junkie runaround.

"He's around," Micky said, waving a hand back toward the neighborhood, looking up at the sky.

I sighed. "When was the last time you saw him?"

"Earlier."

"Today, yesterday, last week?"

He shrugged again.

"I don't have any money," I said. "But when I find him, I can get a shot for you."

"And you'll bring it back here?" He licked his lips. "Right back here to this spot?" He squinted. "You can't tell him it's for me, though." He got serious all of a sudden. "I owe him, and if he knows it's for me he'll never give it up."

"I'm not gonna tell him it's for you. And I don't give a fuck what you got going on with him or anyone else. Just tell me when you last saw him."

"Rat King is always down at the harbor these days. He's been down there most days since you left."

"Really?" Montrose Harbor was where we used to change into our swimsuits in the summer; it was just through the park.

"Yeah. Staring out at the water or the Hancock or some shit."

"Thanks." I started toward the harbor. I didn't know what I would say to him. It hadn't occurred to me until that moment, but I didn't know if he wanted to see me at all.

"You coming back? How long you gonna be?" Micky yelled from the corner. I looked back and saw the string of his yo-yo had snapped. He hung his head for a moment, studied the toy, slipped the string from his finger and tossed it in the gutter.

The walls of the tunnel under Lake Shore Drive were spraypainted with years of love letters.

◆ ◆ ◆

"Good morning." Ms. Rebecca greeted us bright and early as we waited in line for our trays at breakfast. I'd been at Trinity for a couple of weeks by then, and she'd proven herself to be kind and stable, always in the same cheerful mood. I'd seen her comforting the blond-haired boy in her office after his first night with Dominic and Francis.

"Ms. Rebecca," I said while the other boys were shoving eggs and frozen hash browns in their mouths, eyes still low and docile with sleep. "I need to talk with you about something."

She nodded and led me to her office, a small, windowless room with the walls covered in squares of paper with various high heels from a daily "Stilettos" calendar she had on her desk. She sat down, silent, waiting for me to talk.

"There's a boy," I said, sitting across from her with my hands in my lap.

"What's he doing to you?" She leaned in. "Is it Dom or Francis?"

"No. It's not like that. It's a boy from the outs. From my old neighborhood."

She leaned back. "Okay. Before you go on I need to tell you that I'm a mandatory reporter. So if you're in danger I legally have to contact the police."

I sighed. "It's not like that. I shouldn't have said anything."

"Alex, it's okay. I just want you to know the rules I have to follow."

"I've known him since I was little. I really..." I paused and took a breath. "I like him. And, well..." I squirmed in my chair.

"And you don't know if he's like that?" Ms. Rebecca said with a smile.

My eyes pointed to the floor.

"Tell me about him."

I told her about Javier, getting arrested, Montrose Beach and Saturday nights. It felt like confession.

Ms. Rebecca leaned back in her chair and listened, took in all the information. "What are the clues?" She squinted and forced a smile.

"Clues?"

"Yeah. Every man has clues. Don't you know that?" She rolled her eyes.

I shrugged.

"Well, does he look at you like this?" She let her eyelids fall half-shut, pouted her lips a little, and cocked a bit of a smile.

"I don't know what the fuck that is," I laughed.

"Stop it." She patted me on the hand.

"Look, Alex." She got serious. "I know what it's like out there. I know what it's like in here. The first thing you need to do is make sure this Javier stuff stays between you and me." She motioned toward the door. "Some of these kids are animals, and you don't need any more trouble than you've got. Second," she brushed her bangs from her eyes, "if you like the boy and you think he likes you and you just can't live without knowing..." She paused, and I stared at her, waiting for the instruction.

"What?" I said as she leaned back in her chair. "What? What should I do?"

"Get your answer," she said. "Now go on, get out of here. Go watch TV with the others."

I stood up and turned the knob.

"It's going to be alright," Ms. Rebecca said. "I'm proud of you."

I walked through the kitchen and slumped next to Dominic or Francis or somebody with the same expressions and face and movements. It didn't matter who it was. I had a secret now. One that sometimes made me feel like a helium balloon, floating far away to somewhere beautiful, and other times, like a thousand-pound weight sinking to the bottom of Lake Michigan.

"Fuck you," I heard one of the boys say, and Francis slapped him with an open palm so hard the boy feel to his knees. A crowd formed around them. They were all eyes and teeth.

Ms. Rebecca was right. They were animals.

◆ ◆ ◆

Javier was at the harbor, staring into the city as if he'd been waiting all the time I was looking for him, the entire time I was away.

The sun fell and a single star shone above the water. There was no moon. It was strange to see a star and no moon. His eyes stayed locked on the Hancock, the blinking lights on the skyscraper's antennas. The water was still and serene, and his body glowed in the twilight. The sky turned a color I'll never see again.

I sat next to him on the harbor ledge, and we looked into the sky and the water and the distant city lights, letting the air move slowly between us. He laid his head on my shoulder, silent. How long we stayed like that I'm not sure. When I looked up, the moon shone—full and bright like a spotlight—and I knew, for a little while at least, I was home.

◆ ◆ ◆

When I got back to Trinity, Ms. Rebecca was waiting on a sofa in the common room. I thought she'd been waiting for me, and I was about to get scolded.

But as I came closer, I noticed another figure on the couch. The blond boy who'd had his wallet stolen by Dom and Francis sat next to her with his face in his hands, Ms. Rebecca patting him on the back. The boy was silent. He'd either muted his sobs when he heard someone coming or was sitting there dry-eyed with his face in his hands. Either way, there was something eerie about his silence and vulnerability. Ms. Rebecca shot me a half-smile.

"You're late," she said, still patting the boy's back.

I shrugged.

The boy let out a high-pitched whine. A noise neither of us was expecting. Ms. Rebecca's look turned from concern to suspicion.

She turned back to me. "You gonna tell me how it went? I know you wouldn't come in this late unless you had a reason."

I smiled and looked back at the boy, "Maybe some other time," I said, and the boy squirmed and moaned again.

Ms. Rebecca looked at me with concern. "Well, you owe me a story," she said, then mouthed at me to help her with the boy. It looked like he hadn't said a word the entire time he'd been sitting there. Just occasionally the odd moaning noises.

I shrugged and began to walk past. Before I could get to the stairs leading to the basement where the other boys snored in bunk beds, the blond boy's body jumped, head springing erect, and he stood tall from the couch. His eyes were a bright green that almost glowed in the dim light. Ms. Rebecca looked startled. We both knew he was about to do something, and we braced ourselves. He was tall and lean, fists clenched. He stared straight ahead at nothing in particular.

Ms. Rebecca looked concerned, like she'd seen this happen before. Before I came back from downstate, Jon told me it was the quiet ones to watch out for. The loud ones were usually predictable. It was the quiet ones that always lost it.

"Why don't you go to bed," Ms. Rebecca said to the blond boy, still sitting on the couch as if she didn't want to make any sudden movements. "Alex will go down with you." She looked at me for some help.

"Yeah," I said. "C'mon. It's late."

Ms. Rebecca nodded to me as a thank-you, but before she could look back, the boy's fist swung, meeting her nose with a clap like a standing ovation. Ms. Rebecca held her nose as blood began to pour. I moved quickly and hugged the boy from behind.

He didn't put up any type of a fight. The look in his eyes was confused, as if he had no idea what he'd just done. His breath was deep and slow.

Ms. Rebecca stood her ground and took her hand from her face, the blood falling to the floor. She looked at the boy, let him see what he'd done. He'd hit the one person he didn't need to. Not the most vulnerable, but the easiest, the one who surely wouldn't fight back.

"Take him downstairs with you, Alex. We can talk about this in the morning."

I led the blond boy downstairs. He didn't put up any fight or say a word. Ms. Rebecca never took her eyes away or even acknowledged the blood falling from her face.

The boy laid in bed in silence, and I could tell his bright green eyes were still wide open.

By the time we all woke up for breakfast the next morning, the blond boy with green eyes was gone. His stuff was packed, and his bed was stripped to the plastic mattress. No one ever saw him again.

When we came upstairs, Ms. Rebecca was there to meet us with her usual greeting, her face cleaned up as if nothing had happened.

For a moment, I wondered if I'd just dreamed the entire day before. I looked to the common area and saw drops of Ms. Rebecca's blood that stained the carpet.

Dom and Francis crowed and yelled, but there wasn't much too them beyond the bravado. Ms. Rebecca looked at me and motioned at my tray.

The blond boy's seat was empty, and Ms. Rebecca smiled, and my food smelled like shit. By the next day, there would be a new boy in the empty chair. And I'd watch him with new eyes.

The boys shoveled food in their mouths between conversation.

Ms. Rebecca leaned from behind, whispering in my ear, "You owe me a story."

I smiled and nodded. She walked around the table surveying her litter, an occasional word or warning or a smile or a pat on the back. She was all we had to live for, a mother, teacher, and guardian all rolled into one.

I ate fast, shoveled the liquid eggs and frozen hash browns in my mouth. I couldn't wait to get back to the harbor.

Piano Thief

Two men pulled a piano down the wooden porch stairs that led into the building's alley. The piano clunked and banged, old strings ringing—step by step—the burnt tint of old flames climbing up its back. The men hemmed and hawed, took a moment from lifting the weight and looked up at a bright blue sky.

One was short and fat with a porkpie hat, dirty blue shirt with a name that wasn't his stitched to the breast. He was a plump man with large cheeks, scar as long and fat as his belly etched into the artery on his neck. The scar was gnarled and savage. A real scar. The type a man gets as a child or adolescent, carries his entire life. The kind he only gets because somebody meant it to hurt, and he lives through it—maybe a drunk father or mugging gone wrong—and he carries it until he's a short fat drunk himself.

The other man was tall and thin, bright green eyes so defined people could make them out from across the street. They were almost luminescent, following their own path, cocked in both directions like he'd just been hit in the forehead with a hammer. It was a miracle he could see at all.

The skinny man let out a deep sigh, pulled a cigarette from his pocket, and lit it with a dollar store lighter.

"You think it's still in tune?" the fat man asked.

The skinny man shrugged his shoulders, took a deep drag, and let the smoke roll from his mouth. He tapped the piano keys with two fingers, soft sounds floating off with the smoke. This was physically the biggest piece they'd ever taken, sure, but it would also put them on track to something new. A small apartment and enough weight to sell in the neighborhood. They could pay the rent and shoot some of the profits. Just for a little while, until it all cleared up. He thought of jobs and steady paychecks, work programs, the same bed every night. The type of life everybody wanted. It had gotten away from him.

He looked at the fat man, who he thought only saw a quick buck for a hotel room and enough dope for a couple days. He shook his head, thinking if he had to leave him, he would.

◆ ◆ ◆

Ms. Rebecca wore an old baseball cap with a Sox logo from the fifties, a hat she said her dad gave her when she was a kid, to pretend they were still South Siders. It was all black with this big white tube sock embroidered on the front, two large angel wings stuck to its back. There were little gaps in the fabric like streaks, making the logo look like it was flying in the wind.

We were happy to get out of Trinity House. I'd been there about a month at that point, and I left every chance I could.

Ms. Rebecca parked the large cargo van way north of Wrigley, damn near Lawrence.

"Can't we just park at the stadium," Dominic whined, wiping the sweat from his forehead, attempting to fan his face with the neck of a stained white tank top. "We'll be walking forever."

"You think we got money for a valet?" Ms. Rebecca said, smiling. "Nobody from the North Side pays for parking. We'll just find some kids on the corner up here, and I'll give them five bucks to watch the car."

We groaned, making it seem like we were more upset than we really were.

To Dom and Francis, this neighborhood was new territory. They were South Siders, die hard White Sox fans, so they'd never been anywhere near Wrigley.

I'd been on this block a thousand times before, seen Wrigley on almost a daily basis, but I'd never actually been to a game. There were more fans around than I remembered. We were still probably a mile from the stadium. It looked like these people now lived in the area. The privileged, freshly minted college graduates puking in the alleys after the game had migrated further north. It didn't quite feel like home.

"They got air conditioning in there?" Francis asked.

I rolled my eyes. "It's an outdoor park."

"How many dogs we get?" Dom asked.

"How much money you got?" Ms. Rebecca gave him that smile and wink that made us all feel like maybe we didn't want to get out of Trinity House after all. We all knew the warmth she could brew in our adolescent guts with just a smile or quick touch on the shoulder; we knew that after we left, either turned eighteen or got kicked out of Trinity House for something stupid, we might never feel it again. We knew we'd wander like stray dogs to the next phase of our lives. And whatever came next, after we finally grew up, would last a lot longer than these short bursts of love we got from Ms. Rebecca.

"One dog a piece, but you should just be happy you get to see the game. Not everybody gets to go to this series, Cubs-Sox," she said, turning forward, and we all smiled, imagining the relish and pickles and mustard glistening in the sun.

"Sox gonna kill 'em,'" Dom said.

I rolled my eyes. "Not at Wrigley."

Dom scoffed. I looked around to see if I'd recognize anyone, if Javier or Micky or anyone from around the neighborhood would show up on the street. I knew they wouldn't. Not until after the game, to pick pockets of the drunk fans from the northern suburbs. We always waited on the Red Line for them to stumble on. "Taking the train is part of the experience," we'd hear them say as we lifted their wallets or snatched their purses. But really, Javier was too old for this now. He would be a few blocks away on Wilson or Sunnyside, standing on the corner.

I hadn't really noticed until that moment, but the neighborhood was changing. Different people and new shiny buildings growing from the normally vacant lots almost overnight. There were fewer hustlers in the streets; junkies and drunks still littered the neighborhood, but they were being pushed into more palatable places—the parks or the alleys. I didn't even know who the alderman was these days, and no one mentioned him or any type of connections like they had in the past, back when doing an alderman favors could land you and your family cushy city jobs.

It hadn't really been on my mind until that moment, seeing all the office workers in their matching Cubs uniforms: the new North Siders. We passed a glassy apartment building still under construction, its ground-level windows tinted with reflection. I saw myself, still growing but slimmed out. I was getting too old for the corner boy routine. It needed to be bigger now.

The new neighborhood wasn't helping us—surely wouldn't—but I couldn't help but feel like our evolutions were paralleled. It was happening. It was almost time.

◆ ◆ ◆

It was a beautiful instrument. At least four feet tall, the original ivory keys bouncing slightly as they thumped down each step, soft notes of B flat carrying in the wind. The patterns in the upper panel were no doubt hand-crafted. Dizzying twists of vines and leaves wrapped around the instrument like they'd grown naturally from the oak it was made of, rather than polished and crafted by a professional.

"You think," the fat man said again, pushing the piano down another stair. "Once we get this back to the spot, things gonna be okay?"

The skinny man grunted, trying to concentrate. He motioned for the fat man to keep moving. He struggled with the weight, joints creaking. He looked down to the cement and broken glass in the alley. They weren't even halfway down the stairs. He wondered where the time had gone. How did he get so old?

◆ ◆ ◆

"How long of a walk 'til we get to the ballpark," Dom whined. "I gotta piss."

"Watch that language," Ms. Rebecca said. "It's gonna be a walk, and then we have to wait in line."

"I gotta piss," Dom groaned, holding the crotch of his pants like a toddler.

"You're just gonna have to hold it."

"I can't," Dom said, and Francis laughed, puckering his lips and hissing like he'd sprung a leak.

"Cut it out," Ms. Rebecca said.

"Really, Ms. Rebecca," Dom said. "I can't hold it."

"You boys act like toddlers," she sighed. She looked around for a bathroom. "Try the store," she said, pointing to a small corner store on Sheridan. Dom ran, still holding his crotch. "You go with him," she said to Francis, who trotted behind. "And don't even think about taking anything off those shelves. Your pockets better be empty when you get back."

She looked at me and sighed. "Children," she said.

She must have seen my eyes scanning the foot traffic.

"You're from around here, right?"

"Yeah," I said.

"I used to have friends right around here when I was growing up. It was a wild place to be a teenager," she laughed, but caught herself.

"Where did you grow up?" I asked.

"I'm from Rogers Park."

"And you're a Sox fan?" I pointed to her hat.

"Most of my family are still South Siders," she said. "But my dad made the ultimate sin."

"What's that?" I asked.

"He moved up here," she smiled. "He can never show his face in Bridgeport again."

We laughed as Dom and Francis ran back toward us.

"Asshole won't let us use the bathroom unless we buy something," Dom said, his face turning red from holding it in.

"I only have enough money for the game," Ms. Rebecca shook her head. "C'mon." She led us a block back toward the van and ducked us in an alley behind an old building everyone from the neighborhood knew about. "Do your business," she said to Dom.

Dom ran a few feet away behind a dumpster. We stood for a moment before we heard a loud thud, the sounds of strings and keys bouncing, the wheezing of breath.

Two men grunted, swore, and banged what looked like an old piano down the porch stairs of the old place.

"Are they stealing a piano?" Francis asked. It was obvious they were, no matter how absurd. They didn't have mover's uniforms and the place was definitely vacant—boarded up windows, the backside of the brick covered in fading tags.

Ms. Rebecca stood for a moment, confused as the rest of us. One of the men, short, fat with a hat perched on his head, dropped the half he was carrying and it landed with a loud thud. "I can't do it," he said to the other man, who was skinny and quiet. The fat man looked down and saw Dom just cutting his stream below. "Hey kid," he yelled, and Dom looked up. "Come here and give us a hand. I got a twenty if you help us get this down."

Dom started toward the stairs when Ms. Rebecca stopped him.

"Excuse me?" Ms. Rebecca said. The men ignored her, motioning for Dom to hurry up. "Excuse me?" she said louder. They turned, the fat man's face scrunching into a nervous expression, the skinny man's eyes dull and unworried.

"Are you working on the house?" Ms. Rebecca asked.

The two men stood silent for a moment. "I need to move this," the skinny man said. "It needs to get out of the building." He ran a hand over the piano like it held memories, carried something.

"You work for the city? Are you clearing this house or something?"

"This place has been boarded up for at least a year," the fat man said.

"Two years," the skinny man said, his eyes moving up and down frantically in any direction.

Dom raced up the stairs and helped the men carry the instrument the rest of the way down. The job was much faster with the extra hands.

The men stayed silent once they got it to the alley.

"Shit," Dom said, catching his breath, holding his hand out for the money, and I waited for them to tell him to fuck off. These two didn't look like they had a nickel between them, much less twenty dollars to hand off to a kid.

"I'll pay you tomorrow," the short man said, snickering.

"What?" Dom looked confused.

"Give him his money," Francis yelled. "He did his part."

"I'm a little short," the fat man said, pretending to look through his pockets. "Come by tomorrow and I'll have the money."

Dom scoffed, puffed out his chest. "I want my money," he said, and the skinny man shoved him back.

Ms. Rebecca intervened, walking with confidence between them. Francis and I trailing behind. Dom looked nervous after the push, like he welcomed Ms. Rebecca taking control.

"I'm just trying to take these kids to a baseball game," she motioned back toward us, the boys who talked shit all day—walked around Trinity House with our chests puffed out—hiding behind Ms. Rebecca like their mother's apron. "I could care less about you two..." she trailed off for a moment, as if it was too absurd, cartoonish, to say out loud. She snickered, "stealing a piano," but as she laughed, her courage grew. "What gives you the right to take this? You going to try and sell it? I know what you all do in places like this. It's disgusting."

The skinny man grimaced, knowing Ms. Rebecca was not going to be easy to get rid of. I saw at that moment he'd made the decision.

The skinny man held a small blade in his fist. He moved the knife with grace, a sort of dignity: slow and meaningful.

Porkpie hat let out small squeals when the skinny man with crooked eyes pulled the knife. We stood in silence, the piano behind them, perched in elegance at the bottom of the stairs.

"What you gonna do with that?" the fat man said, adjusting his hat as Dom and Francis' eyes got wide and looked around for help. Me and Ms. Rebecca looked straight at the blade.

The fat man was running a hand over his scar, poking a swollen index finger into the soft tissue. He knew how it felt—what the blade was like moving in and out of a body—and the sight of the knife made him shake with fear. We could hear him wheeze from behind Ms. Rebecca. He was now pulling at the scar with his finger.

The skinny man didn't have time to argue, and from the way he spoke, he didn't seem to have the words for it either.

"That's it," Ms. Rebecca said. "I'm getting the police." She motioned for us to follow her back to the street.

"Hold on," the fat man said, and when she turned to tell him to fuck off or maybe just give him one of those smiles and a pat on the shoulder that we all knew would make him feel better, the skinny man punched, really more of a push, slow but with force, moving the blade into Ms. Rebecca's stomach. He didn't smile while he did it. He obviously felt no enjoyment. Stabbing her conjured no emotion either way. For whatever reason, the two men were unwilling to leave without the piano.

Ms. Rebecca stiffened, sucked in air like it was her last breath. She turned back to us, all standing in a line, her eyes large and frightened. She held her stomach like maybe she just had the wind knocked out of her, but I could tell it was bad when she moved to her knees and lay on the ground. She fell soft but with purpose, and that's when the blood began to trickle onto the sidewalk. It moved slow, zigzagging lines along pavement, hit cracks, pooled, and ran to a drain in the alley that I had only ever thought caught rain or piss.

Ms. Rebecca laid flat on her stomach now, arms and legs spread like she was jumping to a belly flop. It took another moment for the blood to start running again, the pressure of her body against the pavement giving us momentary hope that maybe she was okay. It just looked worse than it was, we thought. But the zigzagging lines now pooled under her, seeping out from her body, puddling along in the alley. That's all I could see those first few moments. Then she started to moan. Low, guttural sounds like the sleeping howls of a nightmare.

The three of us moaned along with her. None of us had any idea what to do. We mimicked her sounds and stood frozen. Hoping, praying, that she would stand up and tell us what to do next. The skinny man looked down at Ms. Rebecca, and for a moment his eyes straightened. He turned slowly, like stabbing her was nothing out of the ordinary. He might as well have been tearing our tickets at the stadium.

"Pull," he said to the fat man in a squeal, motioning to the other side of the piano. He looked at the three of us, who now had tears streaming down our faces. He grabbed the other end of the piano, and we watched as the two men who shattered our lives moved slowly away, the scar bouncing on the fat man's neck.

As the two men moved, Dom was the first to regain any consciousness.

"Call the cops," he said, staring down at Ms. Rebecca, who was now quiet, and turned up to the sky. Francis crouched, pressed on her stomach, and she whimpered like a puppy.

The blood was still pouring. I'd seen people stabbed before, but no one who meant anything to me. I'd never known anyone who'd actually died from being stabbed, but this seemed different. My legs began to twitch, and I wanted more than anything to run as far from Ms. Rebecca as I could.

"Go get somebody," Francis yelled, and Dom stood shaking with fear.

The voice was all I needed. I took off running to find a cop or someone to help. There was fear in both Dom and Francis's eyes, tears brewing, knees shaking. I knew that's how I would remember them for the rest of my life.

I ran to Wilson a few blocks away, pointed an officer toward Ms. Rebecca. The overweight cop waddled as fast as he could toward the old two-flat.

I stood there on Wilson and Sheridan for a moment, in front of a new glass apartment, looking out through the neighborhood, the people and the high rises, all the changes since I'd been away. I thought of Ms. Rebecca laying in the alley. Everything I had at Trinity House, in this new life I was trying to build, was bleeding out behind a building I'd walked by every day since I was a child.

My mind slowed, and I thought about how eager I was to run. I could still feel my legs twitching, telling me to get as far away from this as I could. A wave of shame ran through my body. I couldn't take the thought of going back to Trinity without Ms. Rebecca, and I couldn't stand facing her after letting this happen to her. I gave in and began to run toward home. My real home. The only home someone like me would ever really know. My shame turned to anger as my legs pumped, and I decided it was going to be me who left. I was the one with the power now. There would be no more fake families or makeshift parents. It was up to me to choose.

Nothing was going to be good, that was for sure, but it couldn't get any worse than it was at that moment. It was time.

◆ ◆ ◆

I felt like I was going to faint by the time I made it to Montrose Harbor, where Javier sat on a ledge, the rat tattoo crawling up his neck. He handed off a button to Micky who scurried off into the trees. He waved, rubbed his hands together. I walked with purpose, and by the time I got close, his arms were spread wide.

When I finally came to him, our bodies fit together like pieces of a broken bottle, a needle that slips with ease into a fresh vein.

Mother

Ms. Rebecca,

I covered the windows in tinfoil six months ago. The room is completely black except for a small reading lamp set on an old bedside table. Before I just hung up a throw blanket. The fabric was thin, and as soon as the sun poked out over the lake, the light poured into our studio. I'd hear birds singing in the tree outside the window. Their songs always send a shiver down my spine.

Anyone who hears birds sing while coming down off coke, when their jaw aches from bliss and muscles want to pop from tension and die in sleep all at once, knows the piercing sound of birds just when the sky begins to turn.

In the beginning, the tinfoil let me sleep. But I became used to the dark. I spend all night on Broadway and Wilson, in front of City Sport's metal-shuttered doors and windows. Then I come home to the black while Javier sleeps on the couch.

Micky comes to see me on the corner every couple of weeks after a bender, no sleep and he needs to come down. His rotten jaw makes me proud of my full set of crooked teeth. He tells me he needs just enough to knock him out. Not enough to OD. He's not a junkie, he says, he just needs to sleep. He will go back to Howard, to his mother's basement, where the windows are neatly covered with tinfoil, and he can rest. He tells me no light will get through. He will sleep for at least three days.

I haven't seen the sun in six months, since Micky told me about the tinfoil. Now, every day, before the beginning of dawn when the birds wake up, I just drink myself to sleep. Once the dream hit, the one when the needle breaks in my arm, I quit using any downers. I don't even snort it anymore. I've been pouring at least a fifth of vodka down my throat every night. I used to sip grapefruit juice after I pulled from the bottle, but now I just choke it down.

◆ ◆ ◆

Dear Ms. Rebecca,

I never drank red wine. It always seemed like something reserved for the very rich or very poor. I was neither.

But I woke up from the dream, from flipping the car, holding my arm on Javier's handlebars, and it shot out of me, an eruption from the depths of my body. It was heavy, a stream of vomit spattering on the bare mattress. I turned to try and get up, get to the toilet, but it kept coming, pooling on the scuffed hardwood. It smelled sour, tasted like metal. I kept sticking my fingers in my mouth and pulling them out to see the red. I couldn't breathe, panting for air. The muscles in my stomach seized, and my hands turned into claws like I'd just done a shot.

The room was dark, with just that small lamp lit on the bedside table, and I thought I could hear the last chirps of the bird songs from outside the window. I hadn't heard those for a long time.

I couldn't tell where I was before I passed out. All I could feel was the warm pool of blood I'd just thrown up moistening my cheek.

I know you don't want to hear this. You were all I had, still have, and we haven't spoken in years, but I needed to tell someone.

◆ ◆ ◆

Ms. Rebecca:

Plastic veins ran from beeping machines, connecting to my brachial artery. I didn't know you could still get a needle in it. I thought the vein had collapsed a long time ago.

Javier had come home and found me on the floor. We've been living together for a few years but he dragged me to the hall before calling the ambulance. He didn't want the police in our apartment.

He came to see me in the hospital last night, asked when I was getting out. He needed me back, he said. It was hard making enough money on his own, so he'd gotten some new kid, a teenager, to help out, take over my shift, but when the kid came in the morning to give him the money, he was always short, and looked like he'd been nodding off in the alley the past few hours. Good help is hard to find, I guess.

He brought me my journal, promised he hadn't read it. A nurse in her fifties with kind eyes gave me a pen from the pocket of her scrubs.

I told him I wasn't coming back this time. I couldn't take any more. I told him that before the hospital I hadn't seen the sun in six months. I told him about the dream.

He nodded, face stuck in the same neutral expression as when we saw the biker hit. I never grew that face. Unfeeling. Like the whole world could be on fire and from outside everything looks just fine.

He looked away, coughed, the rat on his neck dancing as his throat jerked. I thought I saw him brush away a tear. We sat in silence for a time and he stood up and kissed me on the forehead, gentle, just like he did to Scottie Pippen in the dream, and walked out. I knew that was the last time I'd see him. The last time it would be like it was, at least.

I have a little money, enough for a room for a couple of nights, and maybe I'll get a job, become a person in the world that doesn't shudder when the birds sing.

Shannon

I'd been staying at Shannon's apartment for a week. I slept until noon every day, stayed up drinking with Shannon until three or four in the morning. She woke up earlier than me, fed her kids oatmeal and sent them out to the bus stop. She'd lay in bed next to me after her kids left, staring up at the ceiling, cigarette burning between her knuckles, the gallon of Popov we'd been swilling the night before lying next to her on the floor.

Most days, by the time I woke up, she was passed out, and I'd finish whatever was left of the bottle, telling her later she had drained it all that morning and needed to give me money for another. By midafternoon, we were slurring and stumbling over the cigarette-burned carpet.

When her two kids came in from the school bus, they kicked their boots halfway across the room. The younger boy, Sonny, dropped his hat and mittens and snow pants at the front door, remnants of snow melting into a puddle, turning into a black stain on the carpet. *Second-grader evaporation,* Shannon called it, as if the boy had just vanished into thin air, leaving only an annoying mess behind.

Dakota was in the fourth or fifth grade, a rat-faced kid whose arms were always covered with

Sharpie-drawn tattoos. His long hair feathered at the nap of his neck, bangs swept to one side hanging past his temple, like a teen pop star. *Just like his dad,* Shannon said. Apparently, Dakota's father had been living on the couch (where I now sat ordering the UFC fights on Pay-Per-View) until a few days before I arrived. He'd had too much to drink one night and got rough with Shannon, who had to call the cops. They picked him up on a probation violation and no one knew if he was going to show up that night, or in a couple months or years. The place was tense until the kids went to bed. Every door slammed by a neighbor made them jump, thinking he was back.

Dakota and Sonny were usually pretty exhausted by the time they got home from school, docile after a full day of tormenting whatever poor soul taught them at McCutcheon Elementary. But as the evening set in and the streetlights poured their orangish yellow glow through the broken venetian blinds and onto the dirty carpet, their exhaustion evolved into a delirious rambunctiousness.

They ran and screamed through the living room once the Pay-Per-View fights started, the smell of sour milk from their bodies mixed with cinnamon candy dissolving between their baby teeth, assailing my nostrils every time they passed the couch.

I paid sixty bucks to watch the fights, two men throwing sharp knuckles under thin gloves, biceps flexing around throats until unconsciousness. Blood and guts in a caged octagon.

Dakota tackled his brother, rolling to the floor, a ball of small arms and legs, trying to imitate the two men grappling on the screen.

Shannon came in from the kitchen carrying a plate, dirty blond hair resting on her shoulders, thin tank top wrapped around her body. She wore sunglasses to hide the black eyes and bruises on her face. Anyone with two eyes could see through the dollar-store shades to the violence underneath. A thick tricep bulged under the portrait of Snow White's face tattooed just under her shoulder.

She set the plate of oranges on the coffee table in front of the kids; they were still mimicking the fighters, their bodies blocking the screen.

"Get up," she ordered, grabbing the boy's wrists and pulling them to their feet. They looked at each other, wrists clenched tightly in Shannon's fists, giggling, waiting for their mother to leave so they could keep wasting my sixty bucks.

"You two settle down," she said, releasing their wrists. "Eat your snack and then it's off to bed."

Shannon walked back to the kitchen, and as soon as she left, the two were back on each other, right in front of the screen. I grabbed a slice of orange, sucked on it. It was so tart it made my mouth quiver. When the main card came up, the fighters prancing to the cage in sequenced jackets that looked like Halloween costumes, Dakota had Sonny in a headlock, the second grader's blond curls hanging from his brother's hip to his knee. *He's never had a haircut,* Shannon would brag. She told me one night, after we'd drained a gallon of Popov, that Sonny was just a nickname because of his bright blond curls. I never asked what his real name was.

The two men on the screen touched gloves as Sonny screamed. Dakota was now shirtless, I assumed so his fighter routine would feel more authentic. My patience was running thin. I picked up an orange slice, walked around the coffee table, held the slice to the back of Dakota's head, just at eye level. I tapped him on the shoulder. He ignored me, squeezing his brother's head tighter, prompting a high-pitched squeal. I swatted the back of his head this time, a two-finger slap, and he released the boy, turning around with a grimaced face that looked ready to spit venom. Before he could open his mouth, I squeezed the orange, its acidic juices spraying in a fan straight into the boy's eyes. He scrunched his face back in a double chin, clenching his jaw so I could see the dead molar in the back of his mouth, then screamed, "MOM! MOM!" and ran off to the kitchen holding his eyes.

Sonny looked up at me from the floor. His neck was bright red from the headlock. "You wanna watch the fight?" I asked him, motioning to the TV. He didn't say a word, just ran off to his room.

I walked back to the couch and sat down, threw the slice back onto the plate. The match only lasted forty seconds. TKO in the first round. What a waste of sixty bucks.

◆ ◆ ◆

I'd met Shannon at an AA meeting on Berwyn and Kenmore. From the street the old Methodist Church looked half-cottage, half-castle. The walls were made of rocks instead of brick or concrete. A three-story tower with a witch-hat peak poked above the treetops and greystones that flanked the church.

I went to this meeting every week because the clients from Lutheran Shelter Services always showed up to get their cards signed. The old-timers at the meeting, men and women who had been in the rooms for twenty or thirty years, called all the shelter folks Rums. They filed in heads down, eyes on their shoes, lining up to the table in front where the old guy sat who signed the court-mandated attendance cards.

There would be at least thirty or forty of them and, for good reasons or bad, I could blend in well enough with the Rums that the old-timers wouldn't bother talking to me. The shelter folks knew I wasn't one of them, though. Maybe at a glance they could see me pushing a cart overflowing with garbage bags, but if they studied me for more than a moment, their instincts kicked in. They knew I wasn't built for the streets.

The old-timers sat smiling fangs and cracked jokes under their breath about how fucked we all were. Everyone sucked down coffee and stuffed donuts in our mouths.

Shannon sat next to me in the circle of metal folding chairs, steaming Styrofoam cup in her hand. I knew her already but didn't recognize her at first. Her face was black and blue, mangled from a couple nights before with Dakota's father. She sipped the coffee, letting the zip-up hoodie drop down her shoulders, exposing the top of a tattoo, black hair tied with a red ribbon on her bicep. I recognized the top of Snow White's head.

"Shannon?" I said, poking her shoulder with my finger.

She turned to me with tears welling her eyes, overbite gnawing her bottom lip. "Alex?" she said. "Holy shit." She smiled and hugged me with her free hand. "I haven't seen you since, like, the fourth grade."

That was a lie. I saw her on Wilson and Broadway at least every other day for a few years. She still owed me fifty bucks.

"Are you in the shelter?" I asked.

"Just for the last couple of days. My ex..." She motioned to her face. "My kids are staying with a friend."

I had either forgotten or never knew she had children. I was going to say something else but the old guy at the front with the stack of court cards piled on the table started the meeting.

"You'll get these back after we finish," he announced, patting the pile of cards, and the circle let out a sigh.

After the meeting, I took Shannon to Broadway Chicken and we shared a stack of pancakes, balls of butter melting on top, pooling alongside blueberries. We sat on stools at the tiled counter, surrounded by posters of Broadway plays and musicals, most of which I didn't think had ever been on a Chicago stage.

People came in and out to pick up orders, a couple of homeless guys tried to use the bathroom. They all stared at Shannon's face, glancing at me with a frown or a scoff, as if I'd been the one to fuck her up.

"I had to call the cops," she said, cutting into the short stack with her fork. "It was just too bad this time. I don't think he's out yet. Otherwise I know he'd be back."

I nodded as if I had any idea what she was going through. "You still have your place on Sheridan, though, right?" I said, shoving a wad of the crisp pancakes in my mouth, syrup dripping through the stubble on my chin.

"Yeah, I just don't feel safe there. I can't stand the shelter, though."

"Yeah," I said, running a hand through my hair. "Maybe I could stay with you for the night? Just so you don't feel so worried."

She looked me up and down from the corner of her eye, shoving another forkful of pancake into her mouth.

"Just until you get comfortable again," I said. I was out of money and they were about to kick me out of the Apache Motel on Lincoln. I needed a warm bed. A warm body next to me would be nice, too.

"Where are you staying now?" she asked, no stranger to a man trying to talk his way into her apartment.

"Apache," I told her, popping a blueberry in my mouth.

"I stayed there a few times. It's a real shithole," she said.

"Tell me about it. Look, they're kicking me out, and I got no place else to go. Maybe I can help you out, just stay for a week tops, until you and your kids get settled again."

She sighed and we walked out the door.

Her apartment was only a couple blocks away. When we got inside it looked like a crime scene, random toys strewn across the floor, overflowing ashtray tipped on the carpet, dirty dishes piled in the sink. I didn't know if it was always like this, or if it was all debris from the fight with Dakota's dad.

She laid me down on the couch, threw an old quilt over me, and started walking back to the bedroom.

"Maybe I could sleep with you tonight," I said, and she laughed and walked down the hall, slamming the door behind her.

◆ ◆ ◆

Shannon picked up her kids from her friend's place the next morning. Dakota and Sonny didn't seem to care there was a strange man in their apartment when they got home. They kicked off their shoes and plopped in front of the TV, immediately fighting over the remote.

"I'm Alex," I said to them. They looked at me for a moment, blank expression strewn across their faces. Dakota broke his stare and spit on the carpet, ripped the remote from his brother's hands and began flipping through channels.

◆ ◆ ◆

Shannon put the kids to bed early. She said she was trying to get them back on a schedule for school. It was still light outside when she laid them down.

I ran to the liquor store on Argyle, that one with the blinking neon sign. I bought a gallon of Popov vodka for twelve bucks and a carton of orange juice with Shannon's LINK card. We sipped screwdrivers at first, cracking the window and blowing cigarette smoke through the screen into the cold wind, light snow falling, the flakes so small I could only see them in the glow of the streetlight. But within a few hours we smoked in the living room and pulled straight from the bottle.

◆ ◆ ◆

When I woke up the next morning, Shannon was cracking a new fifth. We drank vodka and ate grilled cheese sandwiches in silence, cartoons blaring on the TV in the living room. I fell asleep again within a couple hours, and when I woke up the sun had set. I could hear her putting the kids to bed in the next room. Shannon gave me a twenty for another gallon of vodka and more orange juice, and we sat on her bed and drank late into the night.

"Get up," she said around two in the morning. She pulled me to my feet. "I used to be a dancer. All growing up. I lived in Boston when I was fourteen, studied at a conservatory."

"I can't dance," I told her.

"You embarrassed?"

I shrugged.

She turned on the radio, moved the dial until she got to the public station. They played classical music all night. The sound of a piano flowed through the static of the old speakers.

"Perfect," she said. "No strings. I always hated dancing to strings."

I shook my head. "No. No. No," I laughed.

"Take off your clothes," she whispered. "It'll make you less embarrassed."

"What?"

She took off her shirt. I saw it wasn't just Snow White tattooed on her shoulder. She had black vines climbing from her hips to her breast, thorns jutting from the stalks. When she turned around to unhook her bra, two small angel wings rested on her shoulder blades.

She slid off her pants and underwear. "Well?" she said.

I undressed, all the way down.

She tried to teach me to pointe and pirouette. I stumbled and she caught me, our naked bodies pressing together. I held her tight, and Leonard Cohen's *Hallelujah* came on. We held each other while the song played, the rattle of Cohen's voice running through our bodies. We began to sway back and forth like two teenagers at a school dance.

I whispered, "I love you" in her ear, and she looked at me, face black and blue, but all I saw was the deep brown in her eyes, a single tear running down her cheek.

We fell on the bed, still pressed together. The old oak headboard banged against the thin drywall that separated us from where her children slept. We only stopped to pull from the bottle and smoke a cigarette.

She fell asleep just before the sun came up, the radio still playing.

◆ ◆ ◆

On the seventh night, after I'd sprayed the orange in Dakota's eyes, the headboard woke her kids up. A slight knocking on the door made us stop. She wrapped herself in a towel and crept to the door. Before she opened it, she made sure I was covered from the neck down with blankets. When she opened the door, Sonny and Dakota just handed her a note and ran back to their room.

She unfolded it, shaking her head as she read the note. I asked her what it was.

"Nothing," she said, folding the paper and dropping it on the dresser. I pushed past her and grabbed it:

Dear Drunk Mom,

We love you and we don't want you to die.

Tell HIM to leave.

- *Dakota and Sonny*

I had never seen anything like it. These fucking kids were really taking a stand. At first I was pissed, thinking Dakota was just trying to get me back for squeezing the orange in his eyes. I read it again, two more times, my heart sinking deeper in my chest. I slid my pants on.

"Where are my shoes?" I asked.

"Where are you going? It's fine. You don't need to leave," she said, pulling from the bottle.

"This is fucked up," I said, flipping to my stomach and looking under the bed. "Where are my shoes?"

"So you're just going to leave now? You're going to run off like a bitch?"

"I can't stay here after that. I'm fucked up, but this isn't the person I want to be. There's a reason I'm not out on Wilson anymore."

"I heard Rat King beat your ass and threw you out after you tried to fuck him," she said, a smile creeping across her face.

"Who the fuck told you that?"

"Oh, shit, so it's true."

I walked to her with my fist clinched, grabbed her by the nap of the neck. "That's a fucking lie," I said. The bruises on her face were healing, fading now. She looked at me like she wanted me to hit her, really beat the shit out of her, kill her maybe. I let go.

"Where are my shoes?" I asked again.

"Fuck you," she screamed, standing up, swinging an open palm that slapped loudly on my temple. She was small but swung like a seasoned boxer. "Get the fuck outta here! Get the fuck out!" she screamed.

I grabbed my jacket, walked down the stairs while she hollered at me from the top floor.

I walked down Sheridan, past Buttercup Park, but Javier wasn't there. I went to our old studio, stood outside and looked up at the old apartment. I couldn't see any light through the window. The tinfoil still covered the glass.

I walked a few blocks down to Montrose, stomped my bare feet on the pavement to the harbor. The entire skyline lit up in the distance. It was so close, but from where I stood, it seemed a hundred miles away.

I dipped my feet in the cold water. They went numb within a couple of minutes. I stared out into the city, full moon shining in the sky, masking a thousand stars. The waves crashed against the cement barrier, splashing up to my knees.

I curled up on the ledges of the harbor. It was the coldest I'd been in my life.

◆ ◆ ◆

I still saw Shannon sometimes around the neighborhood. Most of the time she was with Dakota's dad, the dollar-store shades covering her eyes. He draped his arm around her shoulders, wrist hanging above her chest. I noticed F-I-S-T tattooed on his knuckles. But sometimes she walked with Dakota and Sonny, each child's fingers weaved like wicker in their mother's hand.

Shannon never looked at me when we passed on the street. Sometimes I'd get a quick glance from Sonny, but his eyes would shoot to the sidewalk a moment later. Dakota stared straight ahead with a nasty grimace. Every once in a while, Sonny would look for a beat longer, and I swear the hint of a smile poked from the corner of his mouth, a raise of his eyebrows or a quick shake of his blond curls, cinnamon candy clenched between his baby teeth.

Marathon

I.

She climbed the hill toward the sundial, the last, most difficult leg of her route. Sweat pouring down tan skin, the sun laying heavy on her back, she slowed her pace, reaching the dial enclosed in thick, green bushes, circled by cement benches, wiping her forehead, catching her breath before she stretched.

I sat on a bench about ten feet away, sipping a bottle of water, a cigarette burning between chapped knuckles, backpack perched between scarred knees, stuffed to the zipper.

"You thirsty?" I asked her.

"No thanks," she said, still catching her breath.

"C'mon. I've got another bottle here," I said, holding up the Evian I'd stolen from the restaurant where I washed dishes.

She walked over and took the bottle, cracking the seal, letting the liquid pour down her throat.

"You training for the marathon?" I asked.

She nodded.

"I grew up on the route. My mom and I would set up a table of water every year, wait for the runners to come by."

"Did you ever run it?" she asked, rolling the bottle on her forehead.

"That's too far for me," I said, and she smiled perfect teeth.

A slight breeze picked up, cool, the heat blown away for just a moment as her brown hair floated in the wind.

II.

She'd known me with a stained t-shirt, holes in my shoes, dirty fingernails, months after I dropped out of high school, spending my days crushing Oxys under a dollar bill while my mother worked the late shift. The tip of needle. I didn't live with my mother anymore.

III.

The next time I saw her was after my shift at the restaurant, specks of food from the lunch rush littering my shirt, wet denim soaking my thighs to my knees. It was a busy Tuesday shift. I wasn't expecting any large parties or tables, and I'd forgotten to take the cigarettes out of my pocket. They were still whole, relatively dry, but the flap on top of the pack had all but disintegrated. I picked at the paper, tossing flakes on the street as I made my way to the sundial.

The bushes around the dial were thick, giving the illusion of privacy. It almost felt like I wasn't in public as I unzipped my bag, took out my other set of shorts and a t-shirt, and changed as quickly as possible.

I sat on the bench, lit a cigarette, the filter crooked from my pocket after the lid's destruction.

I waited, two bottles of cold-water sweating in the sun, hoping to see tan skin glistening and brown hair fluttering in the wind. Purple and orange tinted the sky; the dial seemed stagnant. I drank one of the bottles, smoked the rest of the pack, wondering if it was her off day, knowing runners sometimes need to give their body rest.

I saw her ponytail bouncing in the distance, back and forth like a pendulum. I stood with the bottle, a bit of condensation still clinging to the plastic, and she nodded, grabbing the water on her way past.

"Thanks," she called. "I have to go further today. Keep pushing!"

"Keep pushing!" I called back.

IV.

I spent the first afternoon at a movie theater near the university. The matinees only cost a dollar, and there was a film about a guy's last night before he went to prison, how he spent his time, finding out his partner snitched on him, eating his last meal with his family, with his girlfriend, holding each other.

After the movie, I wandered around the neighborhood, watching the students my age carrying backpacks full of laptops and notebooks. I didn't know where to go, so I went to the park right outside of campus; we used to head down here sometimes when skipping class, smoking pot in the trees with my friends before they went off to college.

I came to the sundial, where I'd spent so many evenings passing a bottle of stolen liquor. The stars were out, and I laid my backpack on the cement bench before laying down and stretching my legs. It was cold, before the cicadas sung. A fingernail moon shined among a thousand stars in a dark, low sky that didn't seem so big or frightening anymore.

V.

The day of the marathon people were everywhere. The route ran through the park, near the bench and sundial, a path designated with bright yellow rope and the friends and family of runners cheering them towards the finish line.

I waited, body pressed against the taught, linen barrier, a bottle of water in my hand. Her hair was in French braids, bouncing on her shoulders as her skin glowed in the sun. She pumped toned thighs toward me, reaching for the water.

"Thanks," she said, and her bright green eyes met me with a force that almost brought me to my knees. And I knew, at that moment, without her saying it, without anyone saying it, I didn't even think it, I just knew that I would never see her again. She would probably go off to grad school in a different city in a new state, and I would stay here, waiting on the benches surrounding the sundial.

The spectators cheered as the runners moved towards their destination, towards their victory. Soon they would be on their way home.

Al Pastor

The shots didn't sound like fireworks. It was more like someone hitting a car with an aluminum bat. Ricky said that meant they were cheap revolvers, probably a .32 caliber. "The louder they are the cheaper they are to buy," he said, passing me the joint. "Nobody wants a loud handgun," he shrugged. "What's the point?"

He didn't flinch when the shots rang out, the sound foreign and violent, echoing between brick in the alley behind Carmela's. Meanwhile I almost pissed myself.

"You think it was one of your cousins?" I asked, panting, trying to catch my breath, holding the joint without taking a drag. He laughed.

"Could be. We keep a .32 under the register," he motioned back inside the restaurant. "But I don't think they'd have the balls to use it. If someone was robbing the place they'd just give 'em the money. I mean, it's not like we own Carmela's. It wouldn't come out of our paycheck."

I flicked the roach by the dumpster, and we walked out of the alley toward the front of the restaurant, where Ricky's cousins were watching the lights and sirens pull up. His older cousin, Carlos, was standing with his back leaning against the front window, silent, apron tied around his waist. Alejandro, his younger cousin—who everyone called Andy—was in the crowd, right up in the action.

"Ricardo!" Andy called when he saw us turn the corner. "I was hoping it wasn't your dumbass in the street," he smiled, skipping toward us, excited for all the drama. I don't think I'd ever seen Andy walk anywhere. Saunter, skip, low and slow with a practiced limp, but you'd never catch him walking.

"What happened?" I asked, pointing to the crowd. There were at least twenty cops out now, most just mulling around, trying to look busy, while the paramedics worked on some guy with new Air Jordans in the middle of Lawrence.

"Two guys just started popping off," Andy said with a smile. "This one took it in the head," he pointed a thumb back toward the man in the street.

"Gang shit," Carlos said, running a hand over his mustache, and walked back into Carmela's shaking his head.

I pushed through the crowd so I could get a good look. The man laid in the middle of the street, the paramedics moving him onto a large plastic board before placing him on a stretcher, his head wrapped in white bandage or gauze. There was barely any blood. It wasn't like in the movies where it pooled or splattered everywhere, or they were just cleaning it up as quickly as it came out.

They wheeled the guy to the ambulance right in front of the crowd, like they were showing a prized pig for slaughter. His eyes were closed, mouth parted. His tongue stuck out, bloody and mangled like he'd bit a piece of it off when the bullet hit him. The bandages were just for show. He was dead before the ambulance arrived.

The crowd hemmed and hawed.

"Let me get those Jordans!" Andy yelled from the back of the crowd as they shut the ambulance doors, and Ricky scoffed and shook his head. Some people laughed. Most just walked toward whatever bar they were headed to in the first place, the shooting a minor distraction.

I went back into Carmela's and no one mentioned the man for the rest of the night. We smoked in the alley and drank tequila and shot the shit like any other Wednesday evening. I thought I would dream of him, the man with the Jordans. But it wasn't like that. I didn't even shed a tear.

◆ ◆ ◆

Al pastor was a neighborhood favorite. Ricky and his cousins sliced meat straight off the pork shoulder with long, curved blades that reminded me of the swords from *Lawrence of Arabia*.

The meat rotated on a metal spike, dripping and sizzling, bright red coils surrounding the shoulder. I thought the coils looked like the heat lamps on the train platforms in the winter, where crowds huddled for moments of warmth from the bitter wind. I always had an urge to stare straight into the lamps.

There was a show at the Riv that night. It must have been an indie show. Dyed-blue bangs covered faces with too much eyeliner. All the young white girls shoved the al pastor and tortilla chips between their perfect teeth.

Ricky and his cousins wore red uniforms, nodded and winked at the girls they liked, whispered in low voices as sweat poured from under their matching hats. I didn't have a uniform. I didn't technically work there. They called me in for extra help washing dishes or bussing tables, just the shit they didn't want to do. They paid me out of their tips at the end of the night.

Around nine the kids cleared out, walking across the street to the concert. Once they were gone, all Ricky and Carlos and Andy's friends filed into the tiny restaurant, twenty or thirty of them. "The changing of the guard," Carlos called it with a laugh. They gave me shots of tequila, chased with limes we took from behind the counter.

Carlos was the only one with a key to Carmela's. He locked the door right at ten when they closed, turned up the radio, and everyone drank and lit up right there in the restaurant. When the show got out people started coming to the door, trying to order food, and most of the time everyone was nice about being turned away.

"We're closed," Ricky called with a shot in his free hand and one eye open, counting the cash drawer. As the night went on, the kids kept coming, banging on the glass and begging to be served. Andy finally stumbled to the window—still in full uniform—dropped his pants, and waved his dick at the would-be customers. The crowd of emo kids laughed or ran or just stared with confusion until Carlos or Ricky pulled him down and dragged him toward the back.

"One day," he said as they sat him at a table. "One day they won't laugh." He tossed a lime wedge and it stuck to the window, streaking slowly down the glass.

"Yeah, yeah," they told Andy, "everyone will know your name." And they poured him another drink.

◆ ◆ ◆

The .32 caliber went missing Monday morning. "It's gotta be around here somewhere," Ricky said on his hands and knees, peering under a cooler behind the counter. They'd called me in to wash dishes and make simple orders, take care of any stragglers that happened to come in that early. Ricky and Carlos were too preoccupied searching for the gun to take care of anything else.

"You think Andy took it?" I asked. We had all been thinking it, that he took the pistol to scare someone or play a joke.

Ricky and Carlos looked at each other. "He's got no reason," Ricky said. "He just got paid last night, so he shouldn't need to do anything stupid."

Carlos rolled his eyes. "I don't think it's here. You can take off, Alex." He handed me a ten out of the register.

"I'll let you know if I see it or hear anything about it," I said.

"Good looking out," they said, eyes still searching the space for the gun.

◆ ◆ ◆

Rayan's on Montrose sold the cheapest bottles. There were only a few shelves, no coolers for the beer, not even an air conditioner. In the summer, the door was propped open all day to let the breeze flow in from the lake. Flies and wasps flew in with the wind.

I set a fifth of vodka on the counter. The clerk had a thick beard that ran to his barrel chest. A wasp landed on the glass between us. I jumped as his palm thumped over the wasp, slapping the counter so hard I thought it may crack the glass.

"Aren't you afraid of getting stung?" I asked, and he looked at me, sweat pouring down his forehead.

"Aren't you afraid of passing out face-down in the lake?" He dabbed his face with the collar of his t-shirt.

I nodded, said thank you, and walked toward the harbor. The sun was heavy, and I could smell the dumpsters from the street, but once I got closer to the lake the breeze picked up, and the rays of the sun seemed to blow off into the neighborhood.

I sat on the harbor ledge and watched people walk by, jogging or pushing baby strollers. I cracked the bottle and drank, pulled a lime I'd taken from Carmela's from my pocket, and bit into the peel to cover the taste.

I felt pitiful. I'd left Javier to get away from all this shit, to start again, but it was all just turning back to the way it was before. But this time, I was on my own.

I pulled long and deep from the bottle. I let out a breath, saliva filling my mouth. I swallowed. I had to keep it down. It was the only way I knew to keep going.

◆ ◆ ◆

When I woke, waves crashed above the lower ledges of the pier. The moon was bright, hanging full above the lake. I stood and walked toward Buttercup Park, where I knew the cops wouldn't bother me. They'd let me rest all night.

It must have been late, because the places on Marine were dark, silent, doors locked so tight it was like they never had a visitor. I took a turn and found myself at the old studio apartment. It hadn't been that long ago that Javier and I had lived here, and when I wasn't thinking about it, I always ended up walking by. Tonight the lights were off. I could tell the tinfoil had been taken off the windows. From where I stood the apartment looked cold and dark and quiet, motionless in the still air. I heard he had been picked up, and was in Cook County for the next couple of months. This was all in passing, though. I hoped it wasn't true.

I had that euphoria when you only sleep it halfway off and you're rested enough to be coherent, but my head was buzzing like the glow of a streetlight.

There were usually a couple guys in Buttercup selling dope, hanging out and drinking. But it was deserted tonight, all but a man sitting slumped on a bench, a bottle in one hand, his other arm dangling, the shape of a .32 gripped in the hanging hand.

Normally I would have turned and walked back to the lake, spent the night in some trees, but I recognized his red shirt, the Carmela's hat perched on his head.

"Hey, Andy," I called from the edge of the playground. He didn't respond.

"Andy," I said louder, and his head shot up, confused, like he had no idea where he was.

"It's me," I said with my hands raised. "It's Alex."

He let out a wet scoff and waved the pistol. "Fuck off," he slurred.

"Andy," I said again. "What's in your other hand? I see the gun."

Andy looked down at the bottle of tequila. He laughed and waved me over. We passed the bottle back and forth.

"You know your cousins were freaking out about that gun," I said, nodding toward the pistol still gripped in his hand.

"They're always freaking out. Calling me a bitch, treating me like an asshole."

"They care," I told him.

"What do you know?" he said, one eye open.

"Well," I took the bottle and pulled. "Everybody treats me like shit. The guy at Rayan's today told me to go pass out in the lake."

Andy frowned. “Fuck that asshole,” he said, threw his arm with the pistol around my shoulder.

“What are you going to do with it?” I asked.

I wasn’t scared. Andy was too fucked up to aim straight, and I was too fucked up to care.

“Kill them. Kill me,” he flipped the pistol to his other hand. “I haven’t decided yet.”

“Yeah,” I said, taking another pull of tequila. “I bet they’ll beat your ass if you just try to give it back, right?”

“At least,” he said. “They’ll never let me live that shit down. You know we all live together, right?”

I had no idea.

“On Winthrop,” he said. “It’s a fucking studio! They beat my ass, take my shit, call me a bitch.”

I just listened.

“You know, I’m the only one born here. Those fucks can go back to where they came from.” A tear ran down his cheek. “I’m not like them. I don’t know what it’s like in San Salvador. They call me American.”

I thought it over for a moment. “Remember that guy who took one to the head on Lawrence last week?” I asked.

“Nice fucking Jordans,” Andy nodded.

“You think you could do that to them? To Carlos or Ricky?”

Andy shook his head and let out a sob like a beaten dog. “What am I gonna do?”

I placed my hand on the gun. "I'll take it back in the morning. They'll think it was me who took it."

Andy looked at me, and I noticed he had bright blue eyes. He grabbed me and held me close. "Thank you," he said. His tears soaked through my shirt, and I took another drink from the bottle.

◆ ◆ ◆

Carlos and Ricky didn't do much. They spit in my face, slapped me a few times, and banished me from Carmela's forever. They said if I ever came back they'd use the .32 for more than show.

I still walked by every couple of days, and Andy nodded to me out the window. On the nights I saw him, he'd meet me at Buttercup around midnight, and we'd pass a bottle of tequila back and forth, talk about what he was going to do with his life. He had big plans.

"I've got an uncle in California," he said. "My mother's side. Ricky and Carlos don't know him. I'm moving to Long Beach with him."

"What are you going to do when you get there?" I asked, both of us knowing he'd never make it.

"They have restaurants in Long Beach."

"Yeah," I said. "But how's the al pastor?"

"Probably shit."

"You think? That close to Mexico?"

Andy laughed and passed me the bottle. I drank until the tequila was pushing up my throat, sunk my teeth into the lime for chaser. Andy looked up at the sky—clouds moving slowly—the moon hanging full over of the lake.

Warren Park

1.

You sit on the bed in Amanda's apartment, smoking Marlboro Lights and eating licorice under a popcorn ceiling in student housing across the street from Warren Park. It's a cold February night, and the wind howls through cheap windows. She doesn't have an ashtray, so you use a thin ceramic plate from Dollar Tree. She has a habit of holding her cigarettes for a long time without taking a drag, the cherry covered by a rope of ash that you think, at any second, will fall to the sheets.

"Granny ash," you say, pointing to the cigarette, and she takes a small puff, blowing smoke in the air without breathing it into her lungs, and flicking the ash on the plate. You notice then, and for the rest of your relationship, that she never inhales her cigarettes.

2.

She gives you the bed when she moves to Michigan to get her PhD in some social science. You point out the red stains on the fabric, which Amanda tells you are from wine she spilled before she got sober.

"It isn't from my period," she says, crinkling her nose the way she always does when she wants you to believe her. You hadn't considered that the stains might be menstrual blood.

You accept because you haven't had a mattress in years, not a real one, at least. You've been sleeping on an air bed your mother bought for twenty dollars, which you got drunk and passed out on in your clothes every night for a couple weeks, and you think maybe your keys punched a hole in it while you were sleeping. In any case, the air bed no longer holds air. You're still sleeping on it, though, because it seems like the right thing to do. Either way, the cement floor of your basement apartment is hard and cold.

3.

Your mother had moments of sobriety when you were a kid, and when she was sober, she brought you to the library during the day. You remember riding her hip as she pushes through heavy doors, your head resting on her shoulder, small fingers prodding the moles on her neck.

She sets you in the children's section, where the librarian, a plump woman with thick lenses in her purple-framed glasses and long pearls slung around her neck makes sure the other children share their toys and books.

Your mother sits at a table in one of the study rooms, another woman across from her at the table, two blue books open to the same page. "Studying steps," she calls it. You knock on the glass to get her attention, and when she looks, her eyes are low and dull. She frowns and waves you away.

4.

The library staff always smiles and says hello, even as you get older, in your late teens and early twenties, when you reek of booze and fall asleep on the chairs behind the stacks. They knock on the nearby shelf, quiet at first but growing louder to wake you up.

"You can't sleep here," they say in soft voices.

One of the library staff, a man about ten years older than you, mid-thirties, short with unkept stubble and beady eyes, who wears small frameless bifocals and is missing his two bottom front teeth, suggests you check out a book. The book is thick with a deep blue cover, the same book your mother read in the study rooms when you were a kid.

"Read it," he tells you, and walks back to the circulation desk.

The man who works at the library is named Tyson, and you found out you know his younger brother, Jordan, went to school with him, before Jordan went to prison for robbing a trap house you used to frequent, back when you had money.

Tyson tells you to meet him outside of the library at 6:00, and you both walk to a church around the corner, move silently into the basement, sip cheap coffee from Styrofoam cups while people walk to a podium and talk into a microphone about steps and traditions. At the end of the night, everyone holds hands and smiles and prays.

"Where are you staying tonight?" Tyson asks after the meeting, outside in the cold.

The streetlights are humming, and you see small snowflakes falling in the orangish-yellow light. You shrug your shoulders, "I was at LSSI for about a week, but they kicked me out when they caught me drinking in my room," you say, shocked that what came out of your mouth wasn't a lie.

"You can't stay at my place. My mother has a strict rule against guests staying the night." He thinks it over for a moment. "C'mon." He walks you around the corner, back to the library. He unlocks the door and leads you upstairs to a large conference room on the second floor, and opens a closet door behind a podium that stands at the front of the room.

"You can stay here tonight," he says. "But don't tell anyone I let you in. If they find out, just tell them you snuck in here before close."

You nod, lay down on the thin carpet among stacks of chairs and folded tables.

"Why are you doing this?" you ask.

"You're the first one who actually came to the meeting," he says, closing the closet door.

5.

You ride the bus to the library every day to shelve books. The job is only about twenty hours a week, but it's nice to get the paycheck.

You find the little apartment in the basement of a three-flat a guy in the program owns. "He only rents it to newcomers, people who need a place to stay," everyone at the meetings tells you.

It's small and dirty when you move in, and there's a half-gallon of vodka left in the freezer from whoever rented the place before. They must have been kicked out, you think, as the only stipulations of living in the apartment are a hundred dollars a week and complete sobriety.

Tyson watches as you pour the bottle down the drain. He's there to help you move, but there really isn't much to it. You plug the small air pump into the bed your mother bought you when you saw her a week or so before, the first time you had seen her in months. Tyson brings an old TV his mom was throwing away.

You sit on the air bed while he fidgets with the bunny-ear antenna, crying "Voila!" when the screen finally shows the nightly news.

Tyson sits next to you on the air mattress and you both stay silent for a moment. He puts an arm around your shoulder.

"It's a real shithole," he says, smiling wide.

"Yeah," you say. "And it's all mine."

6.

You meet Amanda at an AA meeting on Clark and Berwyn. She's much shorter than you, bright blond hair and a smile that looks like it was sculpted by an orthodontist. She looks expensive.

"I can see straight up your nose," she says with a giggle, looking up.

You look down at her and smile, handing her a cup of coffee. "You shouldn't go around staring up people's noses," you say, reaching a hand out, and she shakes it with animated vigor.

"What else am I supposed to look at?" she says. "All these tall people walk around with boogers and nose hairs that desperately need trimming. It really isn't right to just force short people to stare into the mess that is your nose."

"I guess I never really thought of it," you say, sipping the coffee.

"That's because you're a tall person."

"So, how's mine?" you stick your neck out and tilt your head, so she has a good view.

"Meh," she said, flattening her hand and tilting it side to side. "I've seen better."

"Rude," you say, and you both smile.

The meeting starts and you take a seat next to each other, and you notice her blue eyes scanning you up and down while people share in the circle. You notice because you're doing the same.

After the meeting, when everyone stands outside on the church steps smoking, Amanda tells you she studies at Loyola.

"The dorms were all full, so they stuck me on Pratt by Western," she says. "It's nice because it's an actual apartment. I don't have to share a room with anyone. But it takes forever to get to campus, and there's no bus that runs on Pratt."

"Walk down to Devon and take the 155," you say, and she rolls her eyes as if you've just told her to hitchhike.

"Warren Park is beautiful, though," you tell her. "There's an *elote* stand by the tennis courts. They're amazing."

"What the hell are *elotes*?" she says, taking a drag of her cigarette, and you gasp and look at her like her hair's on fire.

"That's it," you say, grabbing her wrist and jumping on the northbound Clark bus, taking a seat next to each other toward the middle. You're both silent as the engine hums. You didn't think about the thirty-minute ride to Pratt, or what you two would talk about on the way. Your cheeks are getting red, you can feel it.

"Are you gonna kill me?" Amanda asks, and for a second you can't tell if she's joking.

"Not until after elotes." You both laugh.

You wash the elotes down with cans of seltzer water at Amanda's apartment. You think it's a beautiful place, shiny hardwood floors and windows that let in natural light. She sits close to you on the couch, and after you begin to kiss, she tells you she's never slept with a guy she just met. Not in sobriety, at least. You are going to tell her she doesn't have to, that you can leave, but before you can say it, she takes your hand, gently with the soft skin of her palm, and leads you to her bed.

7.

You meet Javier on Argyle. You haven't seen him in a year or more. You are surprised he contacted you at all. When he called you a couple days before, you almost didn't answer. You were terrified of what he would or wouldn't say. Before you could make a conscious decision, you answered his call, held the phone to your ear, unable to speak. He must have felt the same, because you both sat in silence for what felt like hours, listening to each other breathe.

Javier wears a Fila tracksuit, Nike high-tops, and a thin gold chain. A heavy-looking bag hugs his back. His hair is sculpted into a fresh fade. He walks with a new swagger, but when he smiles, he exposes the missing front tooth. You wondered why he hadn't had it fixed jail. His eyes are heavy, older, like he's aged ten years since you last saw him.

He gives you a hug, wrapping both arms tightly around you, and you're relieved your bodies still fit together the same as they always did. The smell of pomade wafts from his head.

"Good to see you," he says softly into your ear, and you mumble back that it's been too long.

"Let's get some pho!" he says with a smile.

You walk into a small restaurant, and he orders bowls for both of you.

"This is the traditional way to eat it. No need to get the fancy bowls," he says, munching on bean sprouts on the table in front of you.

You two had been in this restaurant a thousand times before, mostly to use the bathroom or hang out because you knew the owner's son from the neighborhood, and she was nice enough to let you cool off in the air conditioning in the summers, or fill up water balloons in the bathroom sink. She stopped letting you in once you were older, after her son went off to college and you and Javier were still running the streets.

You both sit in silence for a moment, and he raises his eyebrows, beckoning you to speak.

"How long have you been out?" you ask, not knowing what else to say.

He sighs. "Just a few days." And he waves a hand. "You remember all the nights we used to be in and out of here? We used to stretch the balloons over the faucet in the bathroom."

"Yours always popped. You tried to fill them up too much."

"Yeah," he smiles and then stares off for a moment, his eyes hard and dull.

The rat tattoo dances on his neck, and for a moment you see him as that young boy who always looked out for you. But he quickly changes back, and from the look in his eyes, gold swinging from his neck, you can see that boy is gone.

"I'm not going back," he says. "That's a promise." The look on his face wonders if you understand the gravity of his transformation, the level at which he has changed.

"It looks like you've made some changes in your life," you say.

He nods vigorously, happy you're noticing.

"So then, what are you going to do?"

The waitress sets bowls of steaming pho in front of you, thinly sliced beef in brown broth with green onions floating on top.

He shrugs and begins to dress his bowl with basil and bean sprouts and jalapenos. "Get a job, I guess."

You stare at him for a second, amazed he could be this serious about anything. For a moment, you think he's come a long way from the boy who was so skinny you could see his ribs through the thin fabric of his tee shirt, a ghost who haunted Uptown's alleys.

"What type of job are you thinking?" you ask him, tasting the pho, strong flavors bathing your mouth. After swallowing the first spoonful, you already feel stronger. It's been a long time since you've had a good meal.

"You're working, right?" he says. "Maybe you could get me on where you're at?"

You think of Javier shelving books and talking with Tyson and checking out patrons at the circulation desk, how out-of-place he'd be. You think about what will happen after he sees his first paycheck and it's nowhere near the money he's used to making. You see the look in his eyes, and you know he's never going to make it.

"Yeah, maybe," you say, knowing this will never happen. "Are you at Preston Bradley?"

He looks at you in astonishment, as if you could think he would ever live there. "The high rise? No, I'm staying at my parents' place."

"They're letting you stay with them?" you ask. You'd seen Javier's parents around the neighborhood, and when they saw you, they glared with disgust. They were poor but proud people. They hated what their son had become.

"Sure," he says. "I'm covering half the rent for the month."

You do not ask where the money is coming from.

You sigh and eat your meal in silence before he pays the tab.

8.

You and Javier walk toward the lake, down a trail to Montrose Harbor. You sit on the harbor ledges, smoking cigarettes and staring out at the skyline. On the way over, you hear the bottles clanking together in his backpack. Your chest bubbles with anticipation of the liquor, the warmth that comes afterward.

He pulls two 40s of King Cobra from his backpack, handing you one. The second the bottle touches your hand, you know you're going to do it. You crack the bottle and let the malt liquor fall down your throat. You think of Tyson and Amanda for a moment. You consider the last three months of sobriety now gone. But that all fades as you cheers the bottles with a man you've known most of your life. Javier pulls long and deep, eyes closed, the rat moving with the skin of his neck as he drinks. He will never be anything other than Rat King.

As the bottles drain, you start to talk about what you two could do together. You were making pretty fucking good money before, you both agree. But it will be bigger this time. Better. You toss the empties in the lake, making your way to Broadway for a few more drinks.

You stop by your old corner on Wilson, where a new boy stands with the same look in his eye as Javier used to have. You look to Javier with a smile, a joke about where you had both been, but Javier looks angry. He walks with a determined pace, swipes the sidewalk for a piece of concrete, and opens the kid's skull.

The boy falls to the pavement, blood draining from his head. He is covering himself in a fetal position as Javier turns out his pockets, pulls off his shoes and shakes them for any content. You both run, not stopping until you reach Rayan's on Montrose.

"What the fuck was that?"

"Fuck that kid. We're taking the corner back."

He shows you the dope and wad of bills from the boy's pockets and shoes. You know at that moment you can never see him again after tonight. You are not built to go back to the streets, and you know Javier will not make it out here much longer.

"C'mon," he says, walking into Rayan's. "Let's get a bottle."

9.

You wake up on the mattress in Amanda's apartment, no idea how you got there. You have no time to get your bearings, consider if you took the train or a bus or got a ride. She is screaming and throwing small fists that hit your face and arms and chest. Her fists are sharp and quick, and while she hits you, you imagine this is what it must feel like to be pelted with rocks. She leaves bruises all over your body and face that will turn dark blue, then yellow when they heal.

You leave her apartment as she's cursing you and saying you're nothing but a worthless drunk. You walk to a bank, take out two hundred dollars. You've just been paid that morning, and you aren't working for another two days. "This is all I'll spend," you think. "Just enough for a couple of bottles, stay drunk for just tonight."

That shit with Amanda was intense, and you need some relief. Maybe you'll stay drunk for a couple of days, until you have to go back to work.

You know this is all a lie. You have no idea when you'll sober up again.

10.

You go to Amanda's college graduation a couple months later, sit next to her parents who look you up and down suspiciously. You've been going back to the meetings. Sometimes drunk, sometimes with a clear head. This is enough for Amanda to take you back.

You wonder if her parents can smell the vodka on your breath, even though you always thought vodka couldn't be smelled after consumption. They know where you and Amanda met, that you work in a library, but they can't know much else, where you've been, all the other shit.

They are old, mid-sixties, with gray hair and sweaters that lay over button-up shirts. They are from Michigan. You know this because they never stop talking about Michigan, how Amanda has been accepted to a highly ranked graduate program in Michigan. Most of all, though, they talk about their lake house which is situated very near the beach on the Michigan side of Lake Michigan. Sometimes, they talk about Amanda's ex-boyfriend, who is attending law school at Wayne State in Detroit. They regularly speak with his parents, who are happily married and raising an apparently wonderful and successful son.

You nod as if you agree how wonderful this boy and Michigan must be. Much better than you and Chicago, of course. Amanda will be very happy back in Michigan for graduate school.

You promise Amanda you won't drink before her ceremony, before meeting her parents. You think maybe you overshot the mark, as you're having trouble concentrating on what anyone is saying, and you just nod and smile, hoping to get through most of the day without having to speak.

You're scared Amanda will know you're drinking, that you brought a couple of airplane bottles to shoot in the restaurant bathroom once this buzz wears off. She told you a couple of weeks ago that if you didn't sober up, you couldn't come with her when she moved for graduate school.

These are your last drinks, you tell yourself as you pour the small bottles down your throat in a stall, Amanda and her parents waiting at a table in the restaurant. It's only enough to get you through the bullshit of meeting her parents.

When you come back from the bathroom, she is scowling.

11.

Amanda doesn't say you won't be moving with her. On the day she is set to move to Michigan, you are packed, just a backpack and a duffel. Only your clothes. She tells you not to bring anything else, that you'll both furnish the apartment together and she mostly wants new stuff anyway.

Later, she knocks on your apartment door, and when you open it, you see the mattress being pulled into the hallway. At first, you're just surprised she's managed to drag it from the moving truck to your apartment by herself.

"Help me out here," she says, and you grab it and pull it across the cement floor into your apartment. "You keep it," she says.

You stand in silence for a while, rubbing the nape of your neck, your bags sitting by your feet.

Amanda starts to speak a few times but stops, eventually deciding what to say.

"In the future," she says, not looking into your eyes. "I want to be in a space mentally, emotionally, financially—someday, at least—where I can have a child. And I need a partner for that, someone who can support me while I'm working late nights and help take care of a baby." Her eyes are welling with tears. "That just isn't you, is it?"

You stand in silence. You want to grab her and hold her and love her. You want to walk with her to her car and ride shotgun to Michigan and get a job and have a nice apartment. But you know, deep down, that if you really care about her, you can't go. You know this life she wants just isn't possible for you.

"I love you," she says, and kisses you for the last time.

You call Tyson and tell him what happened, trying to get the story out in a coherent way between sobs. Most of the time, you're crying so hard you can't speak.

"Did you drink?" he asks you.

"If I was drinking, we wouldn't be on the phone," you say before blowing your nose.

"So, what are you going to do?" he asks.

"I have no idea."

"Good," Tyson says. "Perfect. That's exactly where you're supposed to be."

Advocate

Tyson got into guns when his dad died, and he inherited a .22 pistol his mother said wasn't allowed in the house. He lived in the basement with a drop ceiling, and he stashed the guns in the tiles.

We drove to Wisconsin or Indiana every weekend in the summer to fire the pistols at cans or bullseyes or nothing in particular. Neither of us had ever fired a gun in Chicago, and now it just didn't feel right to fire rounds in Illinois. That time had passed.

"When you were growing up," I asked Tyson. "Did your dad take you out here to shoot?

"He didn't need to. We lived in the country," he said. "Well, not the country, exactly, but we had some land and were able to do pretty much whatever we wanted."

"You're not from here?" I asked.

"Boone County, Iowa."

"What?"

"It's central Iowa, about six hours' drive from here. An old train depot town."

"Okay," I stood and watched while Tyson loaded the clip of the pistol.

"He used to keep this gun locked in a closet under the stairs."

"When did you move here?"

"When I was twenty." He pulled the slide.

I nodded.

"He restocked vending machines at a university in a town about twenty minutes away from where we lived. He was a drunk, bipolar, a real shitshow."

Tyson's dad had died a month or so before. "How'd he go?" I asked.

"They found him under the stairs, where he kept the gun," Tyson said, aiming the pistol at an empty can of Sprite he drank on the ride over. The .22 cracked, light and smooth. I thought it must have moved through his dad's head like Jell-O.

"What about you?" Tyson said, lowering the gun. "Where's your father? You've never mentioned him."

I shrugged. "I'm not sure."

"So it was just you and your mom?"

"No. Not exactly. There was a guy for a long time. His name was Roger."

"Was he your dad?"

"I'm not really sure."

"It sounds like you have a serious resentment for him. That's something that could send you back out. Your father, or whatever you want to call him," Tyson aimed the pistol. "This is something we should probably look into." He let out another shot.

◆ ◆ ◆

A few years ago, I'd been in detox. The nurse came in every hour, removed the plastic vein from the banana bag— a bright yellow concoction of vitamins and minerals—and pushed a syringe of benzos in my blood. It entered my body cold and sharp.

"Can it be a little warmer?" I asked, and the tired-looking nurse—old with kind eyes—told me she was sorry.

"I left my spoon and lighter at home," she said with a smirk.

"Maybe you'll remember it tomorrow," I said.

"Yeah, Klonopin hits better warm. That's what they all say. You want me to filter it through a cigarette?"

"You're a smoker? You really should quit. It's bad for your health."

She frowned. "You're getting to old for this," she said. "It's just not cute anymore." And she walked out to deal with another fuckup.

I laid back and waited to feel like a person again, for the benzos to flow through my body. It started in my chest, stomach. I never knew how tense I was until I felt my shoulders relax. I wanted to talk to the nurse again, apologize or ask what she meant, or just ramble. I pressed the call button, waited and waited, but she never came.

◆ ◆ ◆

They moved me upstairs after a couple of days to sweat it out, to the top floor with the crazies and the rest of the fuckups.

Everybody shuffled around the ward in their gowns and slippers, some muttering to themselves. You could tell which ones had money and which were only there because of state funding. The rich ones were older, hair and beards neatly trimmed with earrings or nice watches. I thought they looked like lawyers or businessmen.

Angelo had a gold stud in his ear and a thin chain dangling around his neck. He smiled a capped canine that shined under the fluorescent light as he pushed a walker, tennis balls covering the walker's rear legs, brushing softly over the polished floor. He spotted me across the room—eyes bright as a nurse pointed me out—and he began the slow journey in my direction. I pretended not to notice him coming, my eyes pointing out the window overlooking the neighborhood. We were closer to downtown—a nicer area. Men and women were coming home from work to their families and dinners, awaiting long nights in front of the TV. The sun was setting a deep orange above them. In an hour it would be lights out on the ward.

Angelo wheeled up close, leaned his elbows on the walker. "Nymphs," he said, smiling, the gold in his mouth flickering. I pretended I hadn't heard him.

"Nymphs," he said louder, tugging on the sleeve of my gown.

I nodded, hoping he'd go away.

"We got nymphs in our room."

"Our room?" I said.

"I'm Angelo Mutti, your roommate," he nodded as if that meant something. "We drew the short straw, buddy. We got nymphs all over the place in there."

I imagined some fantastic hallucination he must have been seeing. Tiny fairies flying around the room.

"You seen 'em yet?" his hand shook with a rhythm.

"Nah," I said. "I haven't seen any fairies or elves either."

He furrowed his brow. "Fairies and elves?" he said, his face serious. "What the fuck are you talking about, kid?" He shook his head. "I don't want any loonies in my room. Nurse!" he called, and the woman at the desk handing out medication ignored him. "Nurse! This kid's got real problems. I don't want him in my room."

She looked at him, shook her head and shrugged.

"Jesus," Angelo grumbled, turning back to me. "Nymphs. Babies. The little baby cockroaches," he said. "They're called nymphs. Our bathroom is full of 'em."

"I took a piss earlier. I didn't see anything," I said.

He rolled his eyes. "Every time, they give me the loonies. This your first time at Advocate?"

I nodded.

"Look. Some of the rooms here got them bad. Don't bring any food in the room at night or they'll smell it and come out of the bathroom. You'll feel these little tickles all over your body while you're sleeping," he said, "and when you turn on the lamp," he ran his palms over his abdomen to indicate full saturation, "you're covered in the little shits. Sometimes their mamas come out too. The last guy I roomed with, about six months ago, a real crazy fucker, he got a big mama roach in his ear while he was sleeping. Dug way down deep," he pointed a finger into his ear canal. "The guy went ballistic. Running all over the room screaming. Can you blame him?" He pursed his lips and shrugged his shoulders.

I stared in horror at the thought of a roach burrowing in my ear.

"They had to call the attending doctor downstairs to come and pull it out with a big pair of tweezers." He mimicked a yank, the motion of extraction. "It took three nurses to hold him down," he smiled and his eyes widened again. "Get this, though," Angelo leaned in close. "The doctor, he was a real prick, man, he held the thing up between the tweezers after he took it out, its legs wiggling and writhing, and he asked the guy: 'You wanna keep it?' Angelo burst into laughter. I stood in silence and watched as he curled his lips and laughed a deep croak. "Hell of a souvenir, right?" he finally caught his breath.

"Anyway, don't bring any snacks in the room. I'm not trying to leave here with any souvenirs other than the godawful bill and a new insurance claim." He turned and pushed off quicker than he came, slippers dragging across the cement. I looked around the ward, under the tables, every speck, piece of lint, edge of a candy wrapper, chip off a Styrofoam cup, moved a bit across the floor like it could be a nymph. I squinted, trying to tell if any of it was actually moving or if it was all in my head.

"Angelo," I called, and he turned around, raised his eyebrows. "Did he keep it?"

He shook his head. "Would you?" and he smiled, the gold in his mouth flashing.

I nodded. He knew I would. Maybe I was a loony, like he said.

◆ ◆ ◆

Tyson's mother had cleared out their basement a few weeks before. He brought over a card table, which was set in the kitchen with two metal folding chairs. He dropped the phonebook on the table. It thumped and shook the old screws.

"He got a last name?" Tyson asked.

"Who?" I asked, pretending to look confused, knowing he meant Roger. He had been asking about him for weeks. His last name, where he was from, if I'd ever met anyone in his family. I always shrugged, changed the subject, but he slammed the phone book down hard enough I knew he meant business this time.

"You know his last name?" Tyson said, pulling out a chair from the card table and sitting across from me. "You don't have to tell me. To be honest, I don't really care what his name is." He fidgeted in the chair. He was really worked up. "But we're leaving no stone left unturned here. It sounds like you have a resentment for this guy big enough to do something stupid, something that could get you killed, or worse..." (Tyson squinted his beady eyes.) "...keeping you fucked up until you get old and gray and more miserable than you thought possible."

I looked at him, considered picking up the phone book and throwing it against his head until the rest of his teeth went the same way as his bottom two. I decided against it.

"Fine," I said, opening to the yellow pages.

"You know the residential listings are the white pages, right?" he smirked.

"I'm not an idiot," I said, flipping to the residential section, having no idea the phone book was organized so logically. The only numbers I ever called were scrawled on random pieces of paper, or napkins, or just memorized. I flipped through the pages, far away from Roger's actual last name, running my finger over the thin sheet. I squinted, chuckled a bit when my finger ran over a name I recognized.

"Right here," I said, pointing to the listing.

Tyson turned the book toward him. "This doesn't say Roger." His face scrunched into a confused mush, and I could tell he was getting pissed. "You didn't say your 'maybe father's' name was Angelo. You said it was Roger."

"I think it's his brother," I lied. I hadn't thought about Angelo in years.

"His last name is Mutti?" Tyson thought it over. "That Italian? Argentinian, maybe? I never met an Italian named Roger."

"Look, I said it's his brother and who are you to tell me otherwise? You think I don't know my own family?"

Tyson smiled. "Okay," he slapped down a paper and a pen on the table. "I want you to write him," he said.

I rolled my eyes. "It's not even Roger. I don't know if this is the right guy."

"It's worth a shot," Tyson said. "And I don't want to read it. I want you to be polite and honest with your possible uncle, and I want you to ask for information about Roger. This is between you and your fake family, so that isn't my business. I just want you to come to peace with all this shit." He sat in the chair with his arms crossed, proud of himself.

I took a deep breath, picked up the pen, and began to write.

◆ ◆ ◆

Angelo wheeled into our room twenty minutes after lights out. I could hear him arguing with the nurses and orderlies in the dayroom on the ward a few minutes before. "I'm an adult. I can stay up as late as I want," and all that shit. He burst through the door, fuming.

"They treat us like we're fucking children," he yelled, and I could hear the staff in the hallway laughing at him. He wheeled into the bathroom and shut the door.

"Any nymphs in there?" I called, having searched the floor earlier, just before lights out when I knew I'd be alone in the room. I found nothing.

Angelo grumbled, flushed and called me an asshole before slowly moving his walker to the window. The sky was still glowing dimly to the west. He looked down at the street.

"I used to live a few blocks from here," he said, placing a hand on the glass to steady himself. "Not anymore."

"Where do you live now?"

"Gold Coast. A nice high-rise with all the bells and whistles."

"What floor?" I sat up on the mattress, the plastic cover crinkling under me.

"Thirty-second."

"I don't think I've ever been up that high."

He turned around, sat in a plastic chair in the corner of the room so he could still look out the window as we talked. "It isn't all it's cracked up to be. The high-rises have all these rules. Condo association fees. Homeowners dues. Bunch of crooks. Worse than me," he said with a smile.

"What do you do?" I asked him.

"Lawyer," he said, and looked at me as if I was an idiot for not already putting that together. "The money's good, but it's a terrible job. I defend the scum of the earth: junkies, killers, wife-beaters." He trailed off at the last one.

"I'm sure they're not all bad."

"Things happen, you know," he said. "Things you never plan on, never dreamed you'd do. But just happen, when you're fucked up, at least. But you know how that is. The way you hurt people."

I thought about Shannon, when her boyfriend was in jail and we were drinking the whole time. Her two kids were little shits, and I was terrible to them.

"I try to defend people who make mistakes, because a trial is the place they'll end up being judged the most harshly. You ever been to jail?"

"When I was a kid. They sent me to this place downstate."

"You got lucky. Juvies up here are worse than county jail. Those kids are animals." He fiddled with the gold stud in his ear. "What'd you do?"

I stayed silent, and Angelo laughed. "Keep your mouth shut. They taught you well. Let me put it this way. Did you mean to do it?"

I thought about it for a moment. "No. I don't think I've ever meant to hurt anyone."

"No one does. Not really. Things happen. People react." He cleared his throat. "Most of the time they're just fucked up." He paused and stayed silent for a moment. "I used to live two blocks from here. With my wife and son. We owned a three-flat, rented the top two floors to students or newly married couples. They were always nice, good people. I drank a lot back then, not as much as I do now, but still enough." His eyes were pointed out the window, out into his old neighborhood.

"I won a case. A big one. This kid, early twenties, your age, he was trying to catch this guy who had killed his childhood best friend, who was a drug dealer in Chatham. The guy I defended wasn't even in the life. He wasn't like the rest of the knuckleheads running around. Good kid. Was about to start college. Anyway, his best friend was killed, the kid that grew up next door to him, who he had known his whole life. That kid, his friend, was a real piece of work. Selling drugs. A shooter in the neighborhood." He glanced over to make sure I was following along.

"So the kid I'm defending goes to his friend's funeral, loses it when he sees his buddy put in the ground. Can't take it, you know? What would you do? What would I do? The kid starts drinking to dull it all out, goes on a serious bender. Everybody in the neighborhood but the cops knew who killed his buddy, these kids that went to the same school as them growing up, who lived just a few blocks away. The kid I'm defending, he finds a pistol—easy in that neighborhood," Angelo let out a soft chuckle. "Drinks himself into a blackout. He heads to the corner where the crew who killed his friend hangs out, and just unloads," Angelo points his hand like a gun and mimics multiple bullets flying. "The kid can't shoot worth a shit. The crew scatters, the bullets are flying in all fucking directions. He doesn't manage to hit any of them, but the houses and apartments behind the target, they got all lit up. A stray ends up hitting a little girl sleeping in her bed, went through her kidney and liver. The kid I'm defending ran off to hide in Nat King Cole Park and passed out. The cops found him asleep.

He was smart enough to ditch the gun before he passed out."

I remembered hearing about the case a few years before. I thought how easily that could have happened to me. Any of it.

"The state really didn't have shit on this kid, other than they found him asleep in a park a few blocks away. So it wasn't too hard to get the case dismissed. I spun it as the cops just hauled in the first black kid they saw and tried to pin it on him. Honestly, that's exactly what they did. They didn't know who he was or what he was doing there. All they know is they needed a kid from the neighborhood to pin it on.

"I go out after I win the case with some other lawyers and we really tie one on. Celebrating. When I get home my wife had already heard about the case. She didn't have the same outlook as me. She was going on about how that could have been our son sleeping and killed by a stray bullet. How I was making the city worse letting these people stay on the streets," Angelo swallowed hard.

"I only remember glimpses of it. How beautiful she was even while I was doing it to her. I remember the pearls around her neck, ripping them off," Angelo stood up so he could see out the window more clearly. "Come here," he said, and I walked to him. "You see that place?" he pointed out into the darkness. "Just a couple blocks. That light."

"Sure, I see it," I lied.

"That's his room. That's my son's room. They still live there. Every time I need to dry out I come here because I can still see the house. See where he sleeps."

We stared out into the blur of the neighborhood, and I imagined his son sleeping in a beautiful room in a wonderful greystone.

"You close with your father?" Angelo asked.

"No. I haven't seen him in a long time."

"He's thinking about you. Every morning when he wakes up and every night before he falls asleep. He's thinking of you." Angelo sat down in the chair, where he stayed the entire night, until the sun poked through the sky and they called us for breakfast.

I went to the bathroom, sat down on the toilet, and wondered if he was right. Even when they weren't here, if parents always thought about their children.

I looked at my feet, long yellow nails above the bleached white floors, and the cockroach nymphs crawled out from the cracks between the toilet and tile, creeping onto my toes and feet and up my legs. I squinted, brushed at them with my finger, still not sure if it was all just in my head.

◆ ◆ ◆

You don't remember me. Why would you? I was just another loony fuck up they made you room with at Advocate who didn't believe the nymphs—not the nurses—really ran the psych ward.

Sometimes I walk around the block you pointed out to me, where you said your wife and kid still live. Every woman that walks by, I look for the pearls. I can only imagine her as you described her, all beat up. I've never seen your wife.

If I could, I'd live at Advocate—with you as my roommate—two weeks out of every month, with shots of benzos every four hours, searching for the nymphs.

You taught me something while we were there, that even if everything is terrible, and you have nothing in life except searching a psych ward for bugs and waiting for the shots, you're still okay. We're all still okay. We react. We do things we never meant to. All of us: kids, parents, junkies and killers and wife beaters.

You're a good man. You're a father.

Farah

The Red Line was packed butt-to-belly after work. I was on my way to the office happy hour. We had the same event every week at the same Mexican restaurant, awkwardly making small talk with my twentysomething coworkers, Big Ten marketing and business majors that spent their days cold-calling. They still chatted about Greek life and their favorite bars from senior year.

I was twenty-six, draped in the standard office uniform, slacks and a button-up with a half-zip jacket to hide the sweat stains under my arms.

By 11:00, after sipping club soda and pretending I cared about college football for a few hours, I was finally heading home. The trains were no longer crowded, just a few college kids and a guy who seemed to be settling in for the night who lit a cigarette and dropped its ash in the aisle. I took a seat, pulled out my phone, and scrolled through a dating app.

I had hundreds of matches that quickly revealed themselves as algorithms, offering a *no strings attached suck and fuck*. All I had to do was click the link below.

Farah was a new match. Her name looked real, or at least a creative choice for a webcam service. Her photo wasn't a stock thumbnail ripped from a porn site. Her skin looked soft and dark in the picture, clashing with bright red lipstick, a leather jacket, and a shirt that said "The Future is Female." The app said she was twenty-three and lived four miles away.

How are you managing this political nightmare? I typed, my stock icebreaker. I stared at the screen for a couple stops, a hint of excitement bubbling in my chest, waiting for a response.

Lots of alcohol, she sent back.

◆ ◆ ◆

Our first date was coffee in Lincoln Square, where Farah told me she was a student at Northwestern studying speech pathology. She still lived at home with her parents and two younger sisters.

When I walked into The Grind to meet her, I noticed long black hair at a booth in the corner, a textbook covering her face. She wore glasses she thought masked a nose too large for her head, a conservative sweater, gold crucifix hanging from her neck. We ordered mochas and lattes, which turned into appetizers at a bar down the street.

"What do you drink?" she asked me at the bar. "I got this round."

"I don't. Alcoholism kinda runs in my family," I said with a bit of a blush.

She squinted, "Okay," turning to the bartender. "One gin and tonic, and one Coke for the lightweight." She smiled.

We left after a few drinks, a quick hug before she got in her car, an exchange of phone numbers and text messages *good night*.

Our next date was a week later, a Friday when the streets were covered with a thin veil of spring snow.

"So, how old are your sisters?" I asked while we waited for our food, her eyes pointed at the table.

"Ten and fourteen," she said, not looking up. "The older one is taking the selective enrollment exam next week, so things have been crazy at home. I've been helping her study."

"What high school does she want to go to?" I asked.

"North Side Prep," she said. "Where did you go to school?"

"Well, that's kind of a story. I went to Senn for a while," I said, trying to avoid telling her I'd only recently received my GED.

"I went to Lane Tech. We had just under five thousand students."

"Yeah, that's a big school. Where all the smart kids go, right?"

She smirked, obviously happy someone brought up the selectivity of her high school.

"Do your parents still live in that area?" she asked as the server placed masala and plates of naan in front of us.

"My mom does. Actually, we live in the same house where she grew up," I lied, avoiding my one-room garden apartment and my mother's nearby studio.

"What?" Farah's eyes grew wide with confusion.

"Yeah, we both had the same childhood bedroom."

"That's crazy. What about your dad?"

"He moved to California about fifteen years ago. He lives outside of LA." I didn't think this one was a lie, exactly. This was the last place I knew Roger lived, but saying "dad" out loud, especially referring to Roger, pushed a wave of shame and anxiety through my body. I looked to make sure my hand wasn't shaking.

"Oh, Los Angeles," Farah said with a smile. "Do you visit often?"

"It's not the LA you're thinking of. He lives in the Inland Empire, out in the desert. I try to visit every couple of years, but you know, he's busy." I decided to change the subject, the story was really getting a little too complex, and I didn't want to trap myself. But it wasn't all lies. I thought about the days in my teen years, in the library looking up San Bernardino and trying to figure out the general area of where Roger might be.

We both ate in silence for a few minutes. I could feel my cheeks turning red as I waited for the conversation to start back up.

"I've never dated a white guy," she blurted out.

I stared at her for a moment.

"Sorry," she said. "I'm just not sure how else to say it."

"Is that a problem?"

She squinted at me. "Not for me. But my parents, they'd really prefer if I married someone from a Mediterranean family..."

"Oh," I said, the word marriage taking me by surprise. "Well, I'd like to meet them sometime. Your sisters, too."

"We'll have to think about how to do that," she said with a smile. "My family can be a bit...guarded."

"Sure," I said, not in any actual rush to meet them. I was a bit surprised by her confidence, that I would be interested to sit and chit chat while her parents judged me just because we'd been out a few times. But I couldn't shake her pause before her glossed lips pushed out *guarded.* It wasn't curiosity so much as intuition. I knew that pause. After Roger left, my mom was never with another man. Not even a cheap date or dinner or a movie. After him, she was guarded.

"Why don't we just see how things go. No rush," I told her, and she smiled, a chewed wad of naan stuck between her teeth.

◆ ◆ ◆

Farah and I started a routine, weekly dates every Friday for about three months.

"We should go to my neighborhood tomorrow," she would say on the phone the night before our date. "We can go to all my favorite spots since I was a kid."

Farah lived in a Jewish neighborhood that had gone through a transition over the last twenty years, an influx of Middle Eastern and South Asian immigration. She grew up a block off the main street that housed the clubs and restaurants.

At the time I didn't know it, but she had decided to keep me around, and had come up with a plan to ease her family into our relationship through neighborhood gossip. We started meeting once a week where everyone would see us eating sumac fries and drinking smoothies from the juice bar at a neighborhood grocery .

Farah's drinks were always pungent: kale, carrots, and beets with extra ginger. I hated ginger. I held my breath as we sat on a bench outside the grocery, heavy fumes from her cup wafting to my face. We'd walk around after we drained our smoothies and sucked the last of the sumac powder from our fingernails.

Farah's black hair ran down the middle of her back, split ends resting on the curve of her hips. On windy days, when the breeze picked up, her hair flew and twisted into a mess across her face, covering her deep brown eyes, only her teeth smiling through.

The foot traffic greeted her in Arabic and Assyrian, inquiring about her mother and sisters who waited a couple blocks away in the family's bungalow. We walked past California Avenue, crossed the line into new territory, to a bakery where we satisfied our sweet tooth with chocolate-covered matzo.

It wasn't long before word got back to Farah's parents that she was walking hand-in-hand with a tall white guy every week.

"They want you to come over," she told me the day before our weekly date.

"Sounds good," I said. "Don't worry, parents love me."

"Right," she said. "Just wear something nice and don't refuse to eat. Eat everything they give you. I should probably tell you in advance, you're the first guy any of the daughters have brought home, and my father is…" (Farah took a breath.) "…protective."

"You're scaring me a little."

"You don't have anything to worry about. You should pray for me, though." She let out an awkward laugh. "There's just a lot you don't know about him, about my family."

"Okay. Like?"

"He's very traditional. He grew up tough, hungry, so when we were kids, if we didn't finish our dinner, he'd pour whatever was left on our head as punishment."

"Jesus."

"He's really protective of us around boys. Men, I mean."

"Well, I'll make sure to be on my best behavior."

"Please do."

◆ ◆ ◆

"We were the first Christian family in this neighborhood," her father told me in the living room the first time I visited the house. I nodded and smiled as Omar talked of his childhood, thick smoke flowing from his mouth as an orange stuffed with flavored tobacco burned on top of the hookah. "I love my neighbors," he said, motioning to an Orthodox Jewish family walking in front of the house. "I never hear shit from them. Just a quick smile and wave. No fighting."

I sat silently, politely, and blew the sweet stink from my lungs.

"When I came here, I couldn't speak a word of English. I just got out of the army back home , and I was working fifteen hours a day at a liquor store on the South Side. They paid us less than minimum wage. We didn't know any better." He shrugged his broad shoulders. "The violence there, especially holidays. Every Halloween we'd have three extra people working the counter just to make sure nobody robbed the place. I saw a guy get pegged in the skull right outside the door a few months after I got here, a quick pop," he motioned with his finger to his head. "Just like that, he fell into a pile on the sidewalk. That's why I never let my kids go trick-or-treating."

I gave him a concerned but neutral look. He was growing old, gray hair clinging to a receding hairline. It was hard for me to imagine him as a young man, mustached, sitting behind a convenience store counter, or later, as he said, riding the back of a garbage truck. He was kind, even though I was penniless. At first, I couldn't believe he was the same villain Farah had told me about, the one breaking up the house, tipping full bowls of soup on his children's heads if they couldn't finish their dinner.

Farah's mother spoke almost no English, even though she had lived on the North Side for thirty years. While we smoked, she set plates of fruit and pumpkin seeds on the table, glass mugs of chai with a mint leaf from her garden spinning on top. She walked back and forth from the kitchen, by a portrait of Saint Charbel Makhlouf, above burning candles, signing the cross each time she passed.

Farah and I were seldom in the same room at her parents' house. She spent her time in the kitchen with her mother rolling *dolma* and chopping parsley, or picking up and dropping off her younger sisters from school or part-time jobs.

Farah's teenage sister pushed through the front door and slammed it behind her as Omar and I smoked and sucked on the seeds. She was stocky, broad shoulders like her father, draped in a uniform from the restaurant where she worked as a cashier. She moved quickly toward her room, saying nothing, eyes on her feet, bangs hanging in front of her round face from a bowl cut.

"Miss America!" her mother yelled; a smile wide across her face.

The girl grunted a high-pitched whine.

"Come here. Meet your sister's friend," Omar said, and I smiled large teeth stained brown from the tea and smoke. We shook limp hands and she scuttled off to the basement.

The youngest poked her head out of the doorway, subtle giggles and nervous squeaks behind brown eyes.

"Come here, *habibti*," Omar called, motioning to her with a strong wave.

She slid bare feet against the hardwood, plopping in her father's lap.

"I'm Alex," I smiled, holding out my hand, and she slid thin fingers across my palm before placing them back over her face, cracks between digits just wide enough for her to see me behind the barrier of her hands.

◆ ◆ ◆

After my first visit, Farah and I started going by the house after fries and smoothies every Friday. Most of the time we'd only stay a few minutes, taking her sisters downtown to ride the Ferris wheel or consider the complexities of abstract art at the MCA. Sometimes, when Farah didn't want to drive, we rode the train downtown, and we all sat together, Farah and I in two bench seats and the girls in front of us, turned around, kneeling on the stained fabric, showing us photos of boys from their schools on their phones, smiles so wide it seemed to push their cheekbones up to their eyebrows. The teenager no longer looked at her shoes when I was around; the younger sister's bashfulness evolved into incessant questions.

"I think we should go bowling tonight!" I proclaimed one Friday evening after we picked them up, mimicking the form of a perfect strike from the passenger seat, and the car erupted in communal groans.

"Are white people good at bowling?" the youngest asked. "Baba watches white people bowling on TV sometimes," and Farah let out a howl. The teenager pinched the younger sister and she crowed with laughter.

"I'm not sure," I said. "I think it was invented by white people."

"Is that why you're so good?" the younger sister asked.

"Egypt," the teenager said, and everyone turned to her. "We learned in school, in history class, that they played bowling a long time ago in Egypt."

"What kind of school do you go to?" I said, and the younger sister giggled.

"CPS's finest neighborhood school. Poorest ward on the North Side," Farah said.

"Okay, fine. What about miniature golf, putt-putt? My mom used to take me every week during our summer breaks. That's a sport I'm really good at."

"Doesn't get much whiter than that," Farah said, and the car burst into laughter.

◆ ◆ ◆

Once a month we didn't take the sisters out after fries and smoothies. We stayed at the house for dinner and spent the evening smoking hookah and eating *kanafeh* swimming in syrup.

"You get that report card?" Omar asked his teenage daughter, a bit of syrup dripping down his chin.

She groaned and unzipped her bag by the front door, carrying a piece of paper back and handing it to him.

"You have Cs in two classes. I told you how smart you are. What are you doing?"

"This boy in my classes," the teenager said. "He keeps bothering me. Whispers things in my ear when we're taking tests."

"What's he say?" Omar asked, leaning in, smoke curling from his lips.

"I don't know. Just stuff, I guess."

"What do you say back to the boy?"

"Nothing," she whined.

"So, you just say nothing all day in class when this piece of shit whispers in your ear?"

"I guess."

"Tell me what you say back. I know you say something back."

"I don't."

He grabbed her wrist, pulling her close, "What do you tell him?"

"Nothing," she cried, her voice squealing. "You're hurting me."

Omar squeezed her wrist tighter, reaching for the lighter on the table. He sparked the wick and held the flame to her fingertip as she squealed.

"What do you do with this boy?" he shouted, and she puckered into a whistle and blew out the flame. He sparked it again; she blew, and again, and again.

The youngest, who was poking her head through the living room door, watching the commotion, pattered her feet into the living room, leaping on her father's back, swatting small hands at the lighter.

"Stop it! Stop it!" she screamed.

Omar released the teenager's wrist, standing up with the girl still attached to his back, both of his hands grasping her thighs so she couldn't drop to the floor. He lumbered toward the kitchen, Farah and her mother now screaming at him to let her go, for her to run to her room and lock the door. Omar turned with his back toward the wall and with one thrust slammed the child, cracking the drywall and letting the girl slip down to the hardwood.

My stomach dropped, but I didn't flinch when he threw her. The sound was familiar. For a second, I remembered Roger, reeking of vodka, body wrapped in a blue button-up with 'Maintenance' stitched on the breast, throwing my mother's head into the drywall as she crumpled to the floor, bits of white paint falling to her sweater. I kept hearing it, the guttural *slap, crack*. The cringe-inducing sounds of actual violence.

The youngest sister curled in a ball as the teenager scurried to the basement. Farah rushed to the weeping girl who was holding the back of her head, picking her up and carrying her to the backseat of her car as if she had done it a thousand times before. I followed Farah as Omar grabbed his keys and walked out the back door, disappearing into the evening to ride out his anger or shame or just be away from his family. He knew Farah would take care of it. She was the mother and father and protector and nurse all rolled into one.

◆ ◆ ◆

Disinfectant panged my nostrils as I waited in the ER. Farah had gone back with her youngest sister. I looked around the waiting room, at the children with bumped heads drying tears, or the others wrapped in bandages. This hospital seemed different. The plants placed around the chairs grew strong. A woman behind the desk smiled at me. I'd never detoxed here before, but it seemed like a nice place to get well.

Farah came into the waiting room, wiping tears from her face.

"She's just about finished," she said, taking a seat in the chair next to me. "You don't have to stay."

We were silent for a moment; her eyes pointed to her feet. I gently rubbed her back.

"It's not the first time," I said, and she looked at me confused. "That I've seen something like this, I mean."

I told her about Roger leaving, the way he was when he lived at home. My mother in her tiny apartment that I'd never actually been to. I told her about growing up and the last time my best friend brought me to a detox. The corners at night. It seemed like a lifetime ago, but it wasn't.

"Did you notice I didn't flinch. When he did it?" I asked.

She nodded, and placed her head on my shoulder.

Years later she would tell me we 'trauma bonded,' and when she said it, I thought of the moment in the waiting room.

Her therapist would say it was sick, that we did something to each other that wasn't healthy, and Farah should leave and start a new life. She'd take off for a couple of days, or I'd go stay with a sober friend. Her face turned red and she'd say something about how she should have listened to her therapist, repeating 'trauma bonded' amid murmurs cursing my entire family line.

I just called it love.

◆ ◆ ◆

Five stitches to the back of her head. No one spoke as we drove from the hospital back to the house. Omar was still gone when we walked through the door. Farah carried the youngest like a toddler to her bed as I waited in the threshold. I could hear their murmurs as they laid together.

Farah kept telling her, "He's not mad at you. He's not mad at you. We can still go out on Fridays."

Her mother walked to the door wearing a nightgown. She came to me, wrapping her arms around my neck, and standing on the tips of her toes to reach my face, kissed me on both cheeks, peppermint on her breath.

She sat me down on the couch in the living room and went back to the kitchen as the teapot whistled. I sat in the dark, thinking of my mother at home, probably passed out in front of the television with a cigarette balancing on the ashtray. Her son with a new family, going through the same shit she had as a little girl. I thought I'd call her that night when I got home.

When she came back, Farah's mother was holding a glass mug of chai in each hand, one spoonful of sugar with a mint leaf swirling on top. She passed the portrait of Saint Charbel Makhlouf, candles burning low, hands too full to sign the cross.

Confession

I went to confession every Sunday, sat in a box with an old man who counted sins like dollar bills. It had to be the same priest every week, seven-thirty in the evening. He moved the same, gravel in his voice, sniffing as I asked forgiveness, slowly raising a handkerchief to the silhouette of a bulbus nose.

I went because I wanted to be a better man so Farah wouldn't want to leave. I went because I wanted to choose her and her family, but there was something left—deep down—like a spark or a match, that made me want to run and scream, shoot up and fight, a Lost Boy in Never Never Land. I thought maybe the priest would snuff the flame. He laughed the first time I came, and I told him about a dream I had a week or so before where I sipped holy water straight from the font at the entrance of the church and became a loving and honest man.

"I don't think that's how it works," he said behind a screen that reminded me of the door on my mother's back porch when I was growing up—a metal cage, or old jailhouse bars.

"After I drank the water I couldn't stop throwing up," I said. "In the dream. When I woke up, I was gagging."

The priest blew a heavy sigh.

"When are you off?" I asked.

"Excuse me?"

"When are you off? You have to have a set time. Some usual hours. You can't just stay in here all night."

"Eight o'clock," he said.

"What time is it now?"

I could see his silhouette check his wrist. "About 7:45."

"Go get some dinner." I stood up to leave the box.

"Maybe you should try communication," he said. "We have services for newlyweds here at the church. If you call the office, they'll give you some information."

"We're not married," I said.

"Then try five Hail Marys and a couple of Our Fathers."

I threw the door shut when I left the booth. I passed the Holy Water font and thought about dunking my hand in for a sip, or bending down and lapping it up like a golden retriever.

I thought that if my dreams were man-made, so was the sanctity of the liquid. I reached in my pocket, felt the rosary beads smooth between my digits. I sat on the pew in the back of the church and started the prayers.

◆ ◆ ◆

Farah and I would lay in bed after making love. I'd fucked a few times in my life, but this was the first time I understood what people meant by "making love." At first, our bodies didn't quite fit together;

awkward movements made for sloppy, self-conscious fucking.

We kept trying, feeling there was something more. Eventually, we learned every joint and fold of each other's bodies, and something beyond fucking grew between us.

Farah taught me sex was a symptom of love, not an end to itself.

The moon covered her breasts and thighs, and when the wind picked up and shook the blinds, the light shined across her face for just a moment, illuminating her eyes and smile. I knew then she had me. I would be any man she wanted me to be.

◆ ◆ ◆

Farah wanted things I didn't know how to get. A two-bedroom apartment with hardwood floors and exposed brick. Drink carts for the kitchen. A dishwasher. A home.

Sometimes, when it became too much for me to imagine such a life, I told her stories about breaking into houses or shooting up, or guys I knew from my old neighborhood, people who—even if she left—I knew I would never see again.

I told her about everyone in my life leaving and how she was just the same. She would leave, too.

"I only know how to take care of myself," I said to her.

"So I'll teach you to love me," she always replied.

But she was human, and I pushed too far. I wanted to be alone for hours every night. I didn't know how to live the way she wanted, to be the man she wanted me to be.

When Farah got angry her mouth puckered tight, eyes becoming sleepy, and her forehead wrinkled. She looked at me with hatred, but not a type I'd known before. The hatred wasn't directly at me or how I'd acted or what I'd done. She hated me because I could hurt her like no one else.

◆ ◆ ◆

The wooden pew was hard beneath my thighs, and my wallet ached my back. It wasn't that the wallet was big or full or anything, my ass was just nearly non-existent, and the slight asymmetry irritated my spine.

"Hail Mary, full of grace…" I counted rosary beads.

I imagined the priest was an old white guy dressed in long robes and a papal mitre. If Farah knew how I imagined him, she would laugh at how selfish I was, thinking I take confession every week from the pope.

"The Lord is with thee…" I rolled the beads between my fingers, an old black-and-silver rosary her mother gave me when she learned I didn't have one, when she asked me "what are you" one night when we came to pick up Farah's sisters, and I nervously spat "Catholic" from my mouth.

"Blessed are thou amongst women…" The beads were cold as the rosary wrapped around my palm, the crucifix dangling across my fingers.

◆ ◆ ◆

Farah's grandfather always spoke to me in Assyrian or Greek, and when the youngest sister told him I only spoke English, he blushed and apologized in choppy English, only to try to talk to me in either language twenty minutes later. He sipped a glass of dark brown liquid, a concoction he claimed had allowed him to live so long—no one actually knew how old he was. When he wasn't sipping, he covered the glass with a piece of old newspaper tinted the same brown as the liquid.

I fidgeted on the plastic-wrapped couch, listening to the girls chatter and roll *dolma* in the kitchen, little cigars of lamb and rice wrapped in grape leaves. I didn't fidget because of the foreign language or having to sit with the old man slipping in and out of a dementia fog, but because it was said Papou practiced black magic. He'd won the lottery three separate times and disappeared for years after every winning ticket, only to return to his eight children penniless.

"He lost all the money?" I asked Farah when she told me the story.

"Every penny."

"So how do you know it was black magic? Maybe he's just incredibly lucky...and very unlucky, too."

She smirked and looked at me as if I was a child who finally learned to tie his shoes.

I was afraid it was true, that Papou really did practice black magic and could see through my nice clothes and fresh haircut, deep down to what I really was.

Papou took a sip from his drink, swallowed hard and deep, twirled at the hair in his ears with an index finger. He motioned for me to come close. I leaned toward him from my seat, the plastic around the couch crinkling.

"Closer," he mumbled in English.

I stood and walked to him, kneeling down so we were face-to-face. He whispered in my ear: "Do you dream of God?"

I said nothing, and all the laughter and chatter from the women in the kitchen fell away.

"If you look at God in your dream," he said in a mumble, "all your hair will turn white." He motioned to his own head of thinning, wiry white hair.

I smirked.

"He may have great things to tell you," Papou told me, and the vinegar smell of his cup wafted to my face. "But there is always a price. There is always a price."

Farah came in the living room, her face turning from light laughter to a serious look when she saw Papou whispering to me.

She spoke to him in Assyrian, her words not meant for me. But I knew what she was saying. *There are some things about us*, she said in poetry, *that will never be meant for him*.

Papou nodded as if he understood and leaned his head back on the chair. He closed his eyes and drifted off. Farah and I looked at each other for a moment.

"He's just a crazy old man," she said, waving a hand to follow her into the kitchen.

I looked again at Papou, who slept with an odd grimace across his face, curious and frightened and at peace. Just like—at that moment—he could see God.

◆ ◆ ◆

The day she left I felt a weight lift off my chest. My narrow shoulders relaxed; I hadn't known how stressed I was the past four years.

"This is it," she said, deep brown eyes reflecting the light of a fluorescent buzz. She had straightened her hair that morning. It sizzled under the hot plates of electric metal. Small hairs, split ends, protruded from her skull in any direction.

Her makeup was done with care, soft brush smoothing her foundation, with a bit of rouge accentuating her cheek bones. She smelled good, like the first dates we'd gone on years ago. Her perfume panged in my nostrils.

"I think you leaving is a good idea," I said, nervously looking her up and down.

She stared at me for a long time, in that way she always did when she was trying to think of what to say, as she never was very good at verbalizing her thoughts.

She didn't need to say it. I could see it in her eyes, the way she neatly packed her bag, leaving just a few specific items behind she would need to return for.

She would be coming back. She'd just dressed up for the occasion.

I wasn't sure if I was happy about it or not. Passion—real hatred—poured from her, just like true love.

She was gone for a few days.

I knew she would be at her parents'. She had plenty of friends in the city, but she was secretive and obsessed with her image. She would never be truthful about how things were for her and her sisters at home, and she would surely never tell them what I had been like before we met. When she left I knew where I would find her.

I still got nervous coming to the house to talk with her. I was afraid Omar would be there, ready to kill me for upsetting his daughter. But he was a strange man with a catalog of unchecked emotions, and he greeted me with a smile and hug.

He waved a hand toward the bedroom, signaling Farah was inside, before plopping down back in front of the television. She was on her parents' bed, the lights out, cuddled in the blankets. I didn't say a word, just slipped under the covers with her and pressed against her body. She turned her head and we kissed gently. The tears still streaming down her face, we laid in bed until her mother burst in with chai, asking what I wanted for dinner. We sat up in bed and Farah blushed, her mother seeing her in bed—their bed—with a boy.

◆ ◆ ◆

After Farah returned and things went back to normal, that's when I started borrowing her car to go to confession every Sunday. I never told her, but every Sunday I stopped by her grandparents' condo on my way to the church and picked up Papou. We rode in silence to Our Lady of Lourdes on Ashland, sitting on the pews in the back of the church, Papou praying or sleeping while he waited for me to ask forgiveness.

I sat next to him and studied the handcrafted statues around the worship hall, a large painting of a flock of children taking Communion on the ceiling. An old mother rocked back and forth on the pew at the front of the church, her son next to her, nodding off in bliss while his mother prayed for his body and soul.

One day Papou let out a breath so strong and deep I thought for a moment it may be his last. I looked back and forth between them, the boy and Papou. I decided that day not to take confession. One of them was seeing God—the boy nodding out, or Papou—and that's all I wanted. There was no point following the rituals.

I led Papou out of the church, and when we arrived back at his condo, his wife of over forty years came to meet us and kissed me on both cheeks, a thank-you for bringing her worthless husband to church every Sunday.

She took the old man's arm and led him to the door, gently guiding him up the stairs, patiently waiting as he shuffled into their home.

I thought I had seen something special. The love and devotion these two had over the years, through all the bullshit and pain and hatred they'd witnessed. They had a devil. But they also had God. And through Papou and Yiayia's lives—no matter how brutal and ugly, impoverished and violent, no matter what losses they had and would suffer—this God never gave them more than they could handle, never too much.

As her grandmother waved from the back steps, I thought Papou didn't know what he was talking about. It wasn't seeing God that made a person's hair turn white.

Yiayia, the matriarch of the family, led her husband into their home. Long, flowing locks of dark black hair trailing behind her.

I closed my eyes in the driver's seat, thinking about all the times I had loved or been loved. I thought of my mother, a long time ago, taking me to the library on weekdays, Roger as a stand-in father. I thought of Javier, from when we were only children to growing up, showing me a connection I'd never know again. Ms. Rebecca, with the stiletto calendar in her office at the halfway house, a makeshift mother for temporary orphans. Maybe I'd finally send her a letter. I thought of Farah, eating lamb and kofta kabab in the dining room of Yiayia's, the moon draping her body as we laid in bed. The smell of her hair and how she always told me, she promised, she would never really leave. No matter how hard it got.

I opened my eyes, pulled down the makeup mirror, and saw my hair still the same chestnut as before. But as I studied my head, I noticed it, on my temple, right above my ear. I plucked out the first gray hair that I'd ever had, studied it, and dropped it to the floor. I was filled with gratitude. Despite my own best efforts, I'd made it this far.

I pulled off to return Farah's car before it got too late and she started calling. She was making mac and cheese for dinner. I knew it didn't matter where we sat, what we ate, or the mood either of us was in. For the first time in my life I could remember, I knew this was it. No half-guessing or planning to run or other bullshit. I was going home.

Acknowledgments

There are so many to thank, and I will surely miss many.

Thank you to my wife, Mary, to whom this book is dedicated, for her unconditional support through the writing process.

To the wonderful Jerry Brennan and Tortoise Books—thank you for your support and for being an incredible press.

Thanks to my brothers Scott, Stephen, and Sean. To my mother, who brought me to the library at least once a week for the first 10-12 years of my life, thank you. Thank you to my father.

To Lena, Helen, Nabil, and Marie—thank you for your support and for loving me like family.

I have so much gratitude for the faculty in the MFA program at Columbia College Chicago, specifically Joe Meno, whose guidance was pivotal to writing this book.

Thank you to Alex Pruefer, George Coyne, and Dylan Weir for their support, inspiration, and friendship.

Last but not least, I cannot forget the magazines and journals that published parts of this book in some form: *Sobotka Literary Magazine* ("Al Pastor" and "St. Jude"), *Barren Magazine* ("Heartbeat"), *Cowboy Jamboree* ("Warren Park"), and *Arkansan Review* ("Farah").

About the Author

Anthony Koranda is a writer and educator who lives in Chicago with his wife and dog. He received a Master of Fine Arts from Columbia College Chicago. His writing has appeared in *Allium, A Journal of Poetry and Prose, Sobotka Literary Magazine, Cowboy Jamboree, Hair Trigger, Arkansan Review, Potato Soup Journal, The Magnolia Review, Barren Magazine,* and *Into the Void,* among others. Find him online at www.anthonykoranda.com.

About Tortoise Books

Slow and steady wins in the end, even in publishing. Tortoise Books is dedicated to finding and promoting quality authors who haven't yet found a niche in the marketplace—writers producing memorable and engaging works that will stand the test of time.

Learn more at www.tortoisebooks.com or follow us on Twitter: @TortoiseBooks.

CPSIA information can be obtained
at www.ICGtesting.com
Printed in the USA
JSHW031814200323
39198JS00001B/1

9 781948 954730

Timeline of Mozart's Life

1751	Wolfie's sister, Nannerl, is born
1756	Wolfgang Amadeus Mozart is born January 27, in Salzburg, Austria
1759	Wolfie learns to play the clavier at age three
1760	Wolfie composes his very first melodies
1762	Wolfie teaches himself to play the violin; Wolfie and Nannerl are invited to play for Empress Maria Theresa in Vienna
1763	Wolfie and Nannerl perform in Germany, Belgium, France, and England; the artist Lorenzoni paints the children's portraits
1765	Wolfie composes his first symphony, Symphony in E-flat, while in England
1768	Wolfie writes his first opera
1770	Mozart hears Allegri's *Miserere* at the St. Peter's Cathedral and writes it out from memory
1777	Mozart falls in love with Aloysia Weber
1778	Mozart writes the Paris Symphony; Mozart's mother Maria Anna dies
1780	Mozart is commissioned to write the opera *Idomeneo, King of Crete*
1782	Mozart marries Constanze Weber
1784	Mozart's son Karl Thomas is born
1786	*The Marriage of Figaro* opens at the Grand Opera House in Vienna
1787	Mozart composes *Don Giovanni*; Papa Leopold dies
1791	Mozart's son Franz Xaver is born; Mozart writes *The Magic Flute*; a mysterious stranger delivers a letter to Mozart commissioning a requiem; Mozart dies on December 5